HER MOST PRECIOUS GIFT

KIMBERLY BLACK

Steepledog Productions
Copyright © 2017 by Kimberly Black
All rights reserved.

Manufactured in the United States of America

ISBN: 1-946846-02-3
ISBN-13: 978-1-946846-02-0
ISBN-13: 978-1-946846-00-6 (Large Print)

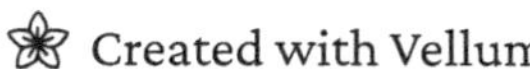 Created with Vellum

DEDICATION

This is for all the beautiful Marys and Marthas in the world. For Tammie, who is the best Martha for my Mary. And for my sister, Lorna, who has always been a sweet Mary to my Martha.

This book is a work of fiction, inspired by Mary, sister of Martha and Lazarus, from the village of Bethany, mentioned in all four gospels of the Bible. While the story is set in a real place, within the framework of real events, it is the product of my imagination. My hope is that my readers will be moved to seek out the message of love and encouragement found within the texts that inspired this novel.

Acknowledgments

My heartfelt appreciation to James Quiggle, for your wisdom, advice, and hours of editing you poured into my this work.

Many thanks to my friends, prayer partners, and beta readers, Kay Stacy, Ron Cleeton, and Sally Wilson, for your honesty, enthusiasm, and support. Endless love and thanks to Tammie Cleeton for standing alongside me as we teach another generation about God's infinite love.

"Martha, Martha, Martha!"

Thanks also to my parents for giving me the wings to use my imagination.

I am especially grateful to my children, Sean, Sam, and Whitney. You three challenge me in the very best way. Most of all, I wish to thank my husband, Riley, for all the ways he loves, serves, sacrifices, and cares for me. Without him, I would never have finished this project.

A very special thanks to Cissy Burch for the never-ending encouragement. And to precious Bailee, for being the face of Mary.

Thank you to Samuel Black, for your work on the lovely cover art for this book.

PSALM 23

A psalm of David.
1 The LORD is my shepherd, I lack nothing.
2 He makes me lie down in green pastures,
he leads me beside quiet waters,
3 he refreshes my soul.
He guides me along the right paths
for his name's sake.
4 Even though I walk
through the darkest valley,
I will fear no evil,
for you are with me;
your rod and your staff,
they comfort me.
5 You prepare a table before me
in the presence of my enemies.
You anoint my head with oil;

my cup overflows.
6 Surely your goodness and love will follow me
all the days of my life,
and I will dwell in the house of the LORD
forever.

CHAPTER

ONE

"It was a lovely wedding feast," Mary said as she followed her brother and sister down the dusty road that led home. "Dinah is a beauty. And Benjamin is a good man."

"Hush," Martha scolded over her shoulder. "Must you carry on all day?"

Mary scowled and slowed her pace. She hoped Martha would notice. When neither of her siblings spoke, she hurried so that they could hear her ask, "Why are you bitter, sister?"

Martha did not even turn her head. "I am not bitter. I am merely sad for Lazarus. If you had any respect for him, you would be sad, too."

Lazarus sighed and joined the discussion. "Do not chide her, Martha. There is no reason for her to be sad. Or you. I certainly am not sad."

Mary smiled at her brother's protective response.

Lazarus had always defended her. She knew, though, that this week had been difficult for him.

"Of course, you are," Martha replied in a tone that sounded very much like their mother's admonitions. "Perhaps not sad, but you must have regrets. After all, Dinah was to be your bride, Lazarus."

Lazarus only scoffed. "Why do you say that?" He shook his head as they all turned onto the path at the edge of their land. "Her father had spoken to me once—a casual inquiry—to gauge my opinion of his daughter." He paused for a moment to face Martha. "As I recall, at the time you were not pleased with the prospect of adding Dinah to our family."

Martha rolled her eyes and walked ahead of Lazarus. "You know that he spoke to our father several times after that."

"Yes, I know," Lazarus said. He directed his words to Martha, but his broad grin to Mary. "He was also interested in learning about our family's income."

Mary took her big brother's arm and leaned into him as they walked. "But you did like Dinah?" she asked.

"I did, yes," he answered. "But Benjamin will make a better husband for her. He is from a wealthy home."

As they reached their tiny house, Mary sighed. "We were a wealthy family once."

Lazarus nodded and squeezed his young sister's hand. "Yes, before the fire."

Mary helped her brother remove his cloak so that he could rest from their journey. She watched as Martha pulled back her head covering and tied a fresh scarf over her hair before turning to the kitchen. Though almost two years had passed, the burn scars that ran from Martha's jaw to her left elbow still turned a bright red whenever she came inside from the sun. Mary wondered how much they hurt her sister. She never dared to ask.

Lazarus patted Mary's arm. "You should go and help her before she scolds."

Mary nodded and tugged her dusty scarf from her head. "Martha, I am going to draw some fresh water," she called out. "Do you need me to bring anything in from the garden?"

She waited for a second but got no reply.

Lazarus raised his thick eyebrows and laughed. "You may be too late. It sounds like she is already in the garden."

Mary hurried to fetch the water jar and then ran out to the yard. Martha sat on her knees, apparently inspecting the cucumbers. Mary approached with caution.

"I apologize for being rude," Mary whispered. "I understand that you only wish the best for Lazarus."

Martha looked up, and Mary could see a hint of red in her eyes.

"I only wish the best for *all* of us," Martha said, reaching for Mary's hand. "It is difficult without mother and father. We are no longer children. We must make responsible decisions for ourselves."

"I miss them, too," Mary said. She wanted to forget about supper and just wrap herself in her sister's arms. She wanted to forget about the fire. She wanted to forget that her parents were gone. That the old house was gone. That everything was gone.

"We must manage without them," Martha said. Her

words were flat and hit Mary in the face with the force of a slap.

Mary flinched and blinked back tears. How could Martha speak like that? Martha was the one person hurt most by the fire, yet she seemed the most unfazed. Mary wanted to shake her. She let her hand slip out of Martha's loose grip, wishing that her sister would hold on just a few seconds more. Martha only shifted her gaze to the cucumbers.

Mary took a deep breath and clasped her arms around the empty clay jar. "I am going for water."

"Hurry back," Martha said over her shoulder.

Once out of sight, Mary let her tears fall. Anger bubbled inside her. She stomped all the way to the well, and by the time she reached the raised stones around the edge, she was gasping for breath. A thick salty stream stained both cheeks and moistened her tunic. She felt like a child in the middle of a tantrum but, as Martha reminded her, she was no longer a child.

Mary turned her eyes up to the heavens. Her weary voice escaped her lips, partly in prayer, but mostly in defiance. "Yahweh, Lord, I cannot take any more. I have no one left but Lazarus. I am a burden to Martha." She knelt at the side of the water jar. "I am a burden to my brother as well. He just loves me too much to speak it." Mary covered her eyes with her palms. "Lord, it would have been better if I had burned in the fire with mother and father, and not Martha. She had a future. She was betrothed. Now she has nothing but worries and pain."

A warm breeze rushed eastward from the hills, and Mary waited as if the wind carried God's voice. When the stillness returned, she sighed and lowered the jar into the well. She let it fill with cool water. Pulling the full pitcher back to the surface strained every muscle in her body. The walk home from Jerusalem had been harder than she thought. Maybe it was that she carried a heavier heart than usual.

She started to raise the jar to her head but then realized she had forgotten to replace her head scarf. She could never balance the pot on her head without it. She released an angry groan and hoisted the jar to her hip.

Mary shook her head as she plodded her way back to the small kitchen. She placed the water jar at the door and went to the basin to wash her hands and wrap up her long black hair. Martha had put on a loaf of bread to bake and was stirring a pot of stew over the fire. Mary found her knife and went to work chopping the cucumbers.

Lazarus peeked into the kitchen and smiled at Mary. She forced a weak smile in his direction, hoping to hide her swollen eyes.

"Is there time for me to speak to Jeb before supper?" he asked.

Martha glanced up from the stew. "Only if you keep to the subject at hand. If you start gossiping, you will be out there all night. You two are worse than old women."

Lazarus nodded and disappeared. Martha returned to stirring. Without thinking, Mary began to hum a song that their mother had sung every evening while the three of them prepared supper. As soon as she realized what tune it was, Mary stopped and swallowed hard, unsure of what to feel. It was the first time she had hummed the song since the fire.

"I hope Lazarus hurries," Martha said. The sound of her

voice startled Mary. "Jeb probably has a great deal to do before nightfall."

"He always hurries," Mary said, defending him. She paused, not wanting to cause any more strife between them. "He loves your stew. He will hurry."

Martha nodded, and Mary accepted that as a sign of truce. Supper was almost ready to serve. Mary sprinkled the oil and spices over the bowl of cucumber pieces. She let the bowl bounce in her hand, flipping the pieces several times until they were coated with the mixture of herbs and oil. She could smell the delicious aroma of the bread as Martha dropped the small loaves into a basket to cool.

Within minutes the table was ready, and Lazarus was back, sitting between his sisters. He raised his palms up, facing heaven, and began to pray. Mary listened to Lazarus's voice, but could not actually hear his words. Her thoughts wandered from the wedding feast to the water well. From Martha's scars to Lazarus's smile. From the fire that took her parents to the fire that burned in her stomach. Mary felt sick. Everything was wrong. Her mother had always offered words of comfort when she was unsure or uneasy. There were no soft words for her today.

"Jeb has three sheep about to birth," Lazarus said, nudging Mary's arm. Only then did she realize he had finished his prayer. The idea of new lambs brought a smile to her face. He continued. "I will take a wagon of lumber and stone to the other side of his property this week. If I stay and help him mend his barn, he will give us the lambs as well as a pair of goats."

"The goats are likely old," Martha said. "And baby lambs require a lot of attention."

Lazarus nodded and sighed. "I can tell him it is too much for us."

"Did I say that we do not want them?" Martha asked. "We have nothing. We must take whatever scraps Jeb is willing to throw."

The knots were back. Mary wanted to scream. Jeb was a friend, and his offer to help should be appreciated. They were not beggars, and Jeb was not treating them like that.

"I will be glad to help care for the lambs and milk the goats," Mary spat out. "This is a good trade. Jeb needs us as much as we need him."

Lazarus grimaced and shrugged. "Martha is probably right, Mary. The goats, the lambs.

They are gifts. Jeb has plenty of material and men to work on his barn. We are a charity to him."

"But he is a friend," Mary insisted.

"And that is why I will accept his offer," Lazarus said. "Mary, we have no more pride. I have lost all standing in Bethany, let alone Jerusalem. We have no money. Our flock is thin. Our fields are barren. Our garden is meager. We live in our old storehouse." He gestured to the walls surrounding them.

Mary dared to look at her sister. Martha stared straight ahead. Her lips formed a thin straight line, and her jaw flexed. Mary felt the rocks becoming heavier in her stomach.

Lazarus dropped his chin, looking ashamed. "The wedding feast this week has served to remind me how I have failed you both. It was my responsibility to rebuild our wealth and find husbands for you."

Martha spoke slowly, with little emotion in her voice. "I will not marry. I was betrothed once. I cannot be rejected again. I would rather take care of you."

"But for her," Lazarus said, gesturing to Mary.

They continued the conversation as if Mary had disappeared entirely.

"What kind of man would want to marry her?" Martha asked. "She is pretty, but she has no dowry estate. If she marries at all, she will be little more than a slave. It would be better if she stayed here with us."

Lazarus sighed. "I will continue to inquire in town, but I fear the prospects are few."

With each word they spoke, Mary felt another brick being set in place around her. Soon a wall surrounded her, and she had no hope of escape. She no longer wanted to scream. She did not have the energy. She had no fight left in her. She swallowed her last bite of stew, but all she could taste was ashes.

That was all they had left after the fire.

CHAPTER

TWO

"Mary, have you left for the well, yet?" Martha called from somewhere outside.

Mary groaned. Of course, Martha knew that Mary was still in her room, dressing for the day. Mary took her time combing out her hair and wrapping it tightly with her head scarf. Lazarus had left for the week, and there would be plenty for the sisters to do without him. She was in no hurry to begin.

"I am almost ready to leave," she called out. "Another trip to fetch water," she mumbled to herself. She thought back to the days when she would follow her mother and one of the house servants to the well. She used to get excited, wondering if they might meet a friend or even a small caravan there. The servants were all gone. The neighbors had long since stopped their visits, and travelers were rare. Now a trip to the well was just another chore.

Mary picked up the water jar on her way out and passed Martha in the garden. Mary could see that Martha had already been working for several hours. Her sister's face was stained with sweat, and her arms and tunic were smudged with dirt.

"Why did you allow me to sleep so long?" Mary asked, glad that Martha had.

"You looked ill last night. I thought you needed the rest."

"Thank you," Mary said with a smile. "I feel better this morning. I will hurry with the water."

Martha nodded, and Mary took the well-worn path toward the hills. She looked up at the wispy clouds forming overhead. Winter had been dry and bitter cold, and spring was ending without the typical rains. Summer would be hot, she suspected. Another hard season and Mary would spend most of it working in their fields. She prayed for help, as she did every morning on her walk.

As she neared the well, she saw two men with a camel approaching from the opposite direction. She slowed her pace. She did not recognize them from Bethany. She wished Lazarus was with her.

"Good morning," the shorter man said. "My master has traveled a great distance and is thirsty. Would you be gracious enough to draw some water for him?"

Mary bowed her head and then glanced up at both men. The servant was already tending to the camel while the other was finding a place on the well's edge to rest. Mary lowered the jar into the well and let it fill. She pulled it back to the surface and poured it into the bowl the servant had retrieved from the pack on the camel. She motioned to the shallow trough on the other side of the well. "May I water your camel, too?" she asked. She recalled the stories her mother had told about Isaac's servant meeting his beloved Rebekah at her family's well.

"How gracious," the traveler said. He motioned to his servant to lead the camel to the trough. "Do you live nearby?" he asked.

Mary blinked in surprise. Men rarely engaged women in conversation. She nodded as she drew another jar of water. "My home is just down the hill from here."

The man took a drink and sighed. "And what does your master do? Does he have business in Bethany?"

Of course, he assumed Mary was a servant. Why not? She was dressed in an old tunic. She wore no jewelry. She winced as she poured out the water into the trough. "My brother owns several fields here. He has a beautiful flock, too." Mary rationalized that there was no need to mention that the fields were bare or that the sheep could be counted on one hand.

"Your brother?" the man replied. "Forgive me, Mistress."

Mary smiled and looked up at the man. His tone and expression hinted that he was teasing. Perhaps he did not believe her. Indignation pushed up into her throat. "My brother is very well respected in Bethany and in Jerusalem," she insisted.

"I am sure that he is," he replied. He took another long sip of water. "I have been away from my home in Jerusalem for several months. My name is Omar. My father is Gad, who owns a caravansary. I have been east, seeking new partners for trade."

Mary nodded and let her eyes meet his. He was a handsome man with sharp black eyes and bronzed skin. His hair was thick with curls, and his smile was broad and white. She noticed his embroidered cloak, finished with blue and gold tassels at the hem. She could not help but return a smile.

"You are very successful, then," she said. "Your family, I mean." She felt a blush rising in her cheeks.

Omar laughed and threw his head back. "Yes, girl, I am." He shot a glance to his servant and back to her. "Like your brother, I prosper at whatever I do."

Now she knew that he did not believe her. A fire sparked in her stomach. "My brother is a great man!" she cried.

Omar set his bowl on the rock beside him and stood. He gestured to his servant, and they both stepped toward her. They each grabbed one of her arms and pulled her away from the well. Mary screamed for help, but she knew that nobody was close enough to hear.

Once the men had dragged her to a clear place among some bushes, Omar pushed her to the ground and dismissed his servant. He knelt beside Mary, holding fast to her arm, and began stripping away her clothes. She continued to scream until he slapped her face.

Mary couldn't think. She couldn't move. Omar pushed himself on top of her and held her face in one tight grip. She tried to turn away, but his fingers dug into her cheeks. He forced his mouth over hers and bit hungrily at her lips. She tasted a salty mixture of tears and blood. She could feel his other hand on her body, and she wanted to die. His attack seemed to last for hours though Mary knew it was only a minute or two.

When he was finished, Omar got up and turned away. Mary used her last shred of energy to hurl a nearby rock in his direction. Though it missed his leg, Omar acknowledged the attempt by spitting on her.

She rolled over and cried into the dirt. Through her sobs, she could hear Omar and his servant plodding away with the camel. She was alone.

In a state of shock and confusion, Mary pulled herself upright and began reaching for the torn clothing nearby. It was covered in dust, as though a great struggle had just occurred. She almost laughed. The idea of struggle implied two equal competitors. What had happened to her was an assault, pure and simple.

She did her best to put her tunic back on, but it was ripped nearly in half. She pulled the loosened scarf from her head and wrapped it around her body, tying it under her arms. She staggered back to the well and found her clay jar shattered on the rocks. *Martha will be angry about that*, she thought.

She looked around, hoping to see someone. She wondered if Martha had even missed her. Omar was out of sight. Mary was thankful for that. There was nobody as far as she could see.

She turned her body toward home, but couldn't take a step. Fear flooded over her, paralyzing her in place. She stared at the path ahead. It seemed to stretch out forever. She wanted to go home but didn't know how. Her feet felt like lead. Her thoughts swirled and her vision blurred. Her stomach flopped over, and suddenly she found herself on her knees, retching air until a stream of vomit poured from her lips. She waited to breathe and then retched again.

When she had nothing left to purge, she stumbled back to her feet. This time, she could move. She walked down the dirt road as if her legs were detached from her body. She couldn't feel anything except for the ache in her head and the dryness of her lips.

"Martha will be furious with you," a voice from far away whispered. "Lazarus will be disappointed. You were their last hope, and now you are worthless."

Mary turned her head to see who was speaking to her, but there was no one. She was alone.

"Why did you talk to him at all?" the voice whined. "You should have turned around as soon as you saw them in the distance."

She stopped in her tracks and looked around again. She turned a full circle, sure that there was someone behind her. No one.

She walked on, and the voice began again. She tried not to listen. It taunted. It accused. It suggested terrible ideas. When she saw her house, she froze. Should she go home? She saw Martha in the doorway, probably watching for her. She could not turn back now. Where would she go even if she did? How could she explain? How could she bear to say the words out loud?

She slowly walked toward the house. She had no other choice.

Martha stepped out into the sunlight. "Where is the

jar..." she started to ask. She stopped abruptly, realizing something was wrong.

Mary shook her head. The voice in her brain quieted.

"What happened?" Martha said, looking her young sister over from head to toe.

"A man," was all that Mary could manage before collapsing into her sister's arms.

Martha dragged her inside the house and helped her to lie down. "Shhh," she whispered. "Do not speak. Just rest for now. I will bring some water."

"Not water," Mary cried out, holding to Martha's hand. "I cannot drink any water."

Martha knit her brows and shook her head. Worry settled into the deep creases on her forehead. "Rest, sister. I will be right back."

"Do not leave me," Mary begged.

"I am not leaving," Martha explained. "I will bring you some wine and bread. You are weak."

Martha pried Mary's fingers from her wrist and went to the kitchen for food. Mary stared at the ceiling, and the voice crept into her brain again.

"See the trouble you have brought to your home? Martha has enough to deal with on her own. Why do you bring her more?"

After several minutes, Martha returned. She brought a food tray and fresh clothing for Mary. She helped Mary bathe and redress, telling her to eat and drink something.

"Sleep for a while, Mary. I will fetch Lazarus. He will know what to do."

"No. I cannot be alone. He is working," Mary sobbed.

Martha stared at her for several seconds, as if in disbelief. "You are hurt," she finally said. "You have bruises all over your body. He will want to know what has happened."

Mary shook her head. "I do not wish him to see me like this. I will rest, and when he comes home, I will be all right."

Martha stood and settled her hands on her hips. "I cannot argue with you any longer. I am leaving to get our brother. Stay here and rest. Do as I say, Mary."

Martha glared with a stubborn slant to her lips. When Mary didn't argue, Martha turned and left the room. A few minutes later Mary heard the latch on the door, and she knew that Martha had left.

Mary sat and stared at the tray of food. She sneered at the bread and couldn't think about eating. She picked up the wine and started to throw it, but stopped. She pressed the cup to her lips and gulped down the liquid as quickly as she could manage. She felt it burn in her throat, probably because of the retching. When the cup was empty, she dropped it back onto the tray and pushed it away.

The voice was gone, and she was tired. Martha wouldn't be back for a few hours.

Mary wandered around her house as if someone had come in and rearranged everything. From the kitchen to the garden, everything seemed different. It was dark, crowded, and dull. She thought about opening the door to let in some fresh air, but when she placed her hand on the latch, a black fear crept into her brain. She thought she heard voices outside. She hurried back to her bed and crawled under a blanket.

Her heart pounded in her chest. Her head throbbed. Her ribs felt crushed. From her hips to her toes, her legs ached.

She heard whispers from the other room, and she began to tremble. She knew that nobody was there, yet she heard them all the same. A multitude of voices, all hissing one word. *Shame.*

CHAPTER

THREE

Mary jumped when the door latch clicked. She held her breath and listened.

"Please, Lazarus, just talk to her. She is frightened. This man, whoever he is, hurt her very badly." Martha's voice pleaded.

"I will speak to her, of course," her brother whispered. "I must also consult a friend of mine. He is a member of the Sanhedrin. He will know what to do."

Mary struggled to swallow. Her throat felt dry and swollen. She wanted to scream, but who would understand? Her brother wanted to tell her story to the Sanhedrin. What would they say? How could that possibly help?

Mary could hear Martha's voice, and she imagined her sister fussing over her brother. "And what will your friend do for Mary?" she asked. "We do not know what kind of influence this man has in Jerusalem. What if he demands her life?"

Mary listened from the other room. She heard Martha's question, and somewhere in her mind, she thought she should be shocked. She wasn't. *What if he demanded her life? What would it matter? Did she even have any life left?*

Lazarus scoffed. "He would never dare such a thing. And by law, he could not."

"He might try," Martha insisted.

Though she couldn't see her, Mary envisioned Martha with her hands on her hips, or possibly waggling her finger in Lazarus's face. She realized that she was wrong when she heard her sister say, "Oh brother, this is my fault. Why did I let her go to the well alone? This is exactly why no woman should ever be unchaperoned."

Mary couldn't let her sister feel guilty for her situation. She rose quickly to join her siblings in the front room, but a rush of dizziness held her in place. She drew a deep breath and released it. Every inch of her body ached. As she lifted her feet to walk, pain shot through her legs and made her cry out.

Martha and Lazarus ran to her. Martha wrapped her arms around Mary and helped her back to the bed. Lazarus just stood a few steps away with his mouth agape. Mary could tell he was shocked at her appearance.

"Oh, my sister," was all he managed to say. He clutched his hands together and shook his head. Mary thought for a second that she could see gray hairs forming at his temples. He suddenly resembled their father. Lazarus took a seat on the stool near the door and let his head sink into his hands. "Yahweh Rapha, hear our prayers," he whispered.

Martha sat beside Mary and studied her face and arms.

Scrapes and bruises covered everything that Mary could see of herself, and she guessed that her face and neck were no different. She felt uncomfortable under Martha's scrutiny, but no more so than from Lazarus's apparent avoidance of her.

"Yes, she needs Yahweh Rapha. She needs a healer. Not just through prayers. She needs a doctor," Martha said.

"And a review by the Sanhedrin," Lazarus replied. "If we are to make this right."

"This will never be right!" Mary cried out. Her own voice was so loud that it scared her as much as it startled her siblings.

Tears flooded over Martha's cheeks and Lazarus stared at his sisters as though he was out of answers. He held his palms up and shrugged.

Mary wanted to cry. She felt her chest heave and a lump rise in her throat. But her eyes remained dry. Her heart pounded loudly in her ears, but tears never came. She dropped her gaze to her hands. Her fingernails were tattered, and her knuckles were scratched.

Her mother used to say that she had delicate hands. Mary almost laughed at the thought. She remembered all the things people once said about her.

"*She has such lovely eyes and radiant skin,*" an echo hummed in her ear. "*She will make a beautiful bride one day.*"

Mary shook her head and covered her ears, trying to make the whispers go away.

"*What a pity it is to see her now. She had such promise. Now she is nothing,*" the taunting voices continued.

"I know that I am ruined! Stop talking and leave me alone!" Mary screamed.

Martha and Lazarus exchanged glances of concern. Lazarus made a fist and pounded his chest in a gesture of anguish. He shook his head, stood, and left the sisters to each other.

Martha watched Lazarus go and then turned back to face her sister. Her eyes shimmered with tears. "We want to help you," she said tenderly.

Mary looked at Martha with a bewildered expression. "I know that." Mary wasn't sure why her brother left so suddenly. "I understand. I am sorry for driving Lazarus away. He must be very disappointed in me."

Martha furrowed her brows. "It is not disappointment, Mary. He is heartbroken for you."

Mary's thoughts began to tumble again. *"You broke his heart with what you did. You should have stopped it. You should have run away. You could have, but you stayed and talked."*

"I never meant for this to happen!" she screamed at the voices.

Martha's chest heaved, and she groaned with obvious despair for her young sister. "Mary, we know," she sobbed. "We know that it was not your fault."

"It was! It was!"

Tears poured out over Martha's cheeks, and she fled the room.

Mary watched as the two people she loved the most left her. She sat on the side of the bed for several seconds, waiting for them to return, but they didn't. *They stayed away. They could no longer stand the sight of her.*

"You have done this," the voices said. Somehow Mary heard it aloud. The echoes were no longer whispers and murmurs. They had found a way to use her own mouth her own throat to speak to her. "You are ruined. You have ruined yourself and your whole family."

She tried to stop the words from forming. She covered her mouth with her hands. Her heart pounded in her ears, and as soon as Mary moved her hands to her ears, her mouth began to move again. "You are nothing but trouble and heartbreak to them!"

She released a long, low moan to smother the sounds of her voice. She coughed for a few seconds after, but the taunting returned. "You did this, Mary. You will never be right again. You will never be clean again."

Martha and Lazarus appeared in the doorway and stared. Their jaws both hung open, and their red-rimmed eyes held pity.

"Look at what you have done to your family. Now be glad that your parents are dead. You should be dead, too."

Martha dropped her head onto Lazarus's chest and pulled the folds of his cloak around her face. Lazarus patted her head and cried. He shook his head from side to side. Mary could see the disdain in his eyes. Disdain she had put there.

She threw herself across the bed and continued to moan. She was vaguely aware that Martha and Lazarus had left the doorway, but she had no idea where they might have gone.

She allowed the tears to continue. They seemed to drown out the threats and accusations. Maybe they didn't, but all

Mary could hear was the sobs. After what seemed like hours, she began to drift off to sleep.

Dreams held little solace for her. She felt darkness and cold all around her and fog shrouded her eyes. Just beyond the gray, someone chased her. She ran, but her feet were slow and cumbersome, and soon she was overtaken by blackness. As she fell on jagged rocks somewhere below, icy fists beat her face and body. Invisible thorns scratched at her legs and tangled her hair. She tried to fight back, but her hands wouldn't obey her thoughts. They only flailed uselessly at her sides as the pounding continued.

She drew in a deep breath as she awoke. Her lungs ached as if she had been screaming for a long time. Her head felt hot, and her body was covered in sweat. She saw the night sky through the window and realized she had been asleep for hours. *Good. You cannot hurt anyone if you are asleep.*

She looked around the room and saw Martha in her bed. She appeared peaceful, finally. Mary sat up in her bed and looked through the doorway into the main room of the small house. Lazarus sat at the table with a lamp burning low. Mary could see that he was rocking forward and back, just a fraction of an inch either way. She knew this meant he was praying.

"For you, no doubt," a voice whispered. *"He cannot deal with you in any other way. He seeks answers in prayer. He will take you tomorrow to the Sanhedrin, and you will be stoned in the streets for your sin. Then it will be over."*

She watched a second more, trying to resist the whispers. They would not be ignored. They took her own voice again. "You will get what you deserve," she heard herself say.

Lazarus looked up. He reached out and gestured for her to sit beside him at the table. Mary nodded and entered, holding her gaze on the flame from the lamp.

Her brother kept his tone quiet, not wanting to disturb Martha. "Mary, my sweet Mary," he began. "I am worried about you. Your sister and I want you to be healthy. We want you to be happy."

"But something must be done." The flame flickered as she spoke.

"Yes, we cannot leave you in this state," he said.

"Broken."

"You have been hurt. Badly hurt." He reached out for her hands.

Mary shifted her eyes to stare at his open palms stretched across the table. She made no effort to put her hands in his, but he left them there anyway.

"We want you to be healed," he said. "We want our beautiful sister back as she was."

Mary shook her head and jumped back to her feet. Her sudden movement bumped the table, and Lazarus reached out to catch the lamp from tipping over. He flinched at the heat and drew his arms back around him.

Mary shuddered at the idea of fire hurting anyone else in her family. "Your beautiful sister is gone. She was stolen from you. This is all that is left. I have nothing but pain and trouble for you now."

Lazarus shook his head. He clearly had no response to her. Martha appeared again in the doorway. Tears already stained her cheeks.

"Mary," she said, her voice shaking. "Come back to bed. You need rest. Tomorrow will be better. You will see."

Mary obeyed, but only because exhaustion was weighing down on her mind and body. She plodded back to her bed and allowed Martha to help her get comfortable. Martha used a damp towel to dab at Mary's forehead. The cool against her hot skin felt calming.

Martha began to hum a song that her mother had sung to them when they were all children. The melody seemed to banish the other voices, and Mary relaxed enough to drift to sleep. But the nightmares quickly returned.

FOUR

Mary woke for the eighth or ninth time to find the sun shining. Martha still sat at her side, humming and patting her hand. She could hear Lazarus outside, preparing for the day.

"Good morning," Martha said. "You got a little bit of rest. Your face is not quite as swollen as last night."

Mary sat up and faced her sister. Her sides still ached, and her head pounded from a night of bad dreams and crying. "Thank you for caring for me."

"Of course, I will always take care of my beloved sister," Martha said with a sigh. "I love you."

She reached out to put her arm around Mary's shoulder, but that was too much. Mary pulled back and frowned. "I am too much trouble. You should not have to take care of me."

A look of helplessness settled back into Martha's expression. "I just want to help you."

"Nobody can help me. I am ruined."

"You are not ruined, Mary. You are hurt, yes. But you are precious to us." Martha held up her hands as if to surrender. "Tell us what you need."

"I just need to die."

Martha burst into tears and ran into the other room. Lazarus came in from the garden, and they began to talk.

Though their conversation was hushed, Mary listened carefully for as long as she could. "We have no other options, sister," she heard Lazarus say.

"But what if the Sanhedrin decides she is to blame? We cannot allow them to find her guilty. She could be punished." Martha's tone was filled with worry.

"I will take her to Nicodemus. I trust him to understand. Besides, the law states that if she is guilty of anything, then this man, Omar, would suffer the same punishment. He may have influence with the Sanhedrin. I should take her torn clothing as evidence, in any case."

"We both know well that the law is not always followed to the letter. A man's authority and testimony carry much more weight. They will punish her and never bring him to judgment at all," Martha stated.

Lazarus nodded. "And that is why I will appeal to my friend. He knows Mary. He knows all of us."

Mary listened to her siblings. Lazarus sounded sure, but Martha had doubts. Mary had very few doubts. They would pronounce her guilty. She would be executed by nightfall. Stoned just outside the gates of Jerusalem. *The gates I walk through every week.*

"Perhaps Nicodemus can make Omar see reason. Maybe he will offer to take Mary for his wife," he suggested.

Martha pounded a fist on the table. The sound startled Mary.

"Do you hear your own words?" Martha cried. "He might have killed her. And yet you would consider allowing him to touch Mary again?"

Mary's heart pounded. She couldn't process anything Martha said. Her thoughts still caught on Lazarus's idea. *I cannot marry Omar.*

"No, no, I suppose that would be cruel," he conceded.

"I cannot believe you would even consider it," Martha said. Mary could hear her pacing the floor. "And what if Nicodemus suggests that? Would you allow it then, or will you champion Mary?"

"I will stand up for Mary."

"Will you?" Martha asked, pushing for a more definite answer.

"I will."

Mary suddenly found herself standing in the doorway. She couldn't remember getting to her feet or walking, but there she was. "You should not risk the shame of presenting me to the Sanhedrin," she told them. "I am not worth the trouble. I can just stay out of sight from now on. I will not disgrace you by going to market again, or anything else. I can become a servant of this house." *You are not even worthy of that.*

Martha and Lazarus shook their heads and went to her side. "You are not a slave. You are our sister," Lazarus insisted.

"And we will never be ashamed of you," Martha said. "We will not allow another evil to touch you."

"The evil is already a part of me," Mary said flatly. Her face showed no hint of sorrow or anger—no emotion at all. She merely stated the fact as she was certain of it. "I will never be right again."

Martha was careful not to pull too hard as she took Mary's arm and led her back to their room. Mary studied her older sister's grave face as Martha began to help Mary wash and dress for the trip to Jerusalem. *She does not have any idea what to do with me. She is going through motions, longing for her routine.*

Martha combed Mary's hair and then gently twisted it into her head scarf, tucking the ends into the roll of fabric at the back of her head. Mary sat still. Her voice was silent, but her thoughts screamed through her mind. She couldn't help but believe that today would be her last. In some ways, that thought gave her a sense of relief. At least, the voices that crowded her head might finally stop.

She looked through the window as Martha tied a loose belt around her waist. Clouds were forming over the hills toward Jerusalem. *Perhaps the sky will weep at my death.*

FIVE

Martha and Mary sat quietly at the entrance to the Court of Women of the Temple in Jerusalem. Martha watched as mothers, daughters, and sisters flowed into the yard to pray. Mary stared at her hands.

Martha usually wore her headscarf with a loose veil to cover her burn scars, but today was the first day that Mary had veiled her face, too. Martha advised that keeping her scratches and bruises concealed would be better for a while. Mary hated wearing the veil. It felt stifling in the heat of the late morning sun.

Mary kept her gaze down as friends and acquaintances greeted them in passing.

It wasn't long before Mary's mind buzzed. *"They can see that you are spoiled. You will never be welcome in the synagogue again,"* she heard.

Martha shot her a glance that told her the voice she

heard was her own. Mary frowned and concentrated on the stones under her feet.

After half an hour Lazarus returned, accompanied by his friend, Nicodemus.

The older man gestured to a cool place under a nearby olive tree. "Let us sit and talk."

Once they were all seated comfortably, Nicodemus asked Mary to pull back her veil. When she did, he winced at the abrasions across her swollen cheek and jaw. He nodded, and Martha helped her replace the fabric covering.

"I see," he said to Lazarus. "And you say the man who did this was Omar, son of Gad?"

Lazarus nodded. "Yes, how well do you know him?"

Nicodemus crossed his arms over his chest. "I do not know him very well at all, but I know Gad. He is a proud man. Very wealthy. His opinions carry much weight with some of the other men in the Sanhedrin."

Lazarus sighed. "What do you suggest?"

Nicodemus looked at Martha, then Mary, then back to Lazarus. He shook his head. "I would recommend that you tread carefully. I want to be fair. Your sister has suffered." He dropped his hands to his lap and turned his face to the sky as if he was requesting wisdom directly from God. "I believe what you say, but if the matter is brought before the whole council, they will not only look at her appearance and torn clothes, but the witnesses' testimony will also be considered. Mary's account will certainly not be verified by Omar or his servant."

"Then this man is permitted to break the Law of Moses

and take advantage of any woman he wishes without being held responsible?" Lazarus asked.

"I wish I could give you more hope."

Mary watched as her brother's face seemed to grow older before her eyes. She despised herself for the trouble she had caused.

Lazarus drew a deep breath and squared his shoulders. "I want to speak with Gad and Omar about the situation. Perhaps I can reason with them."

"And if they bring the matter to us?" Nicodemus asked. "He could push for your sister to be punished. At the very least he could charge you with false witness. I am but one vote. I may be able to sway another, but the whole council would be involved. I doubt my influence extends to such a broad reach."

"I have nothing of any value that they could take," Lazarus argued.

Martha inhaled sharply and fixed a worried expression on her face. Mary knew that she longed to speak.

Nicodemus seemed to notice it, too. He patted Lazarus's arm. "My brother, you have two lovely women who depend on you to live. You have property, however barren it may seem. You have a roof over your head. If they managed to take any one or all of those things from you, where would you be?"

Martha nodded silently and squeezed Lazarus's hand.

Mary chewed on her lips, fighting the accusations that only she could hear. *You are nothing, girl. You cannot speak; you have no sway, not even with your family. You have no voice at all.*

"I have a voice!" she answered loudly.

All three of the others stared at Mary in shock. Tears poured once again from Martha's eyes and soaked through her veil. Lazarus pleaded with Nicodemus. "This is what she has become, now. My sister has been taken over by this. . . this. . ." his voice trailed into sobs. "Nicodemus, what other recourse do I have?"

The man's chin trembled for a second. Mary thought she might have seen a trace of pity in his face. *Surely for Martha and Lazarus. Not for me.*

"If you feel that you must confront Omar and Gad with this evidence, then I will go with you, my friend." Nicodemus nodded as he regarded the torn clothes. "We should go today. Now, if you can."

Mary and Martha followed behind the men as they walked the dusty street to where the caravansaries were found.

Mary had been fighting with her voices, sometimes aloud, sometimes in whispers, always with a feeling that everyone around her could hear. They all seemed to glare in agreement with the taunts and torments. Her legs grew sore from walking, and she tried to stop several times. Each time she slowed her pace, Martha would wrap her arm around her shoulder and push her along.

"I do not want to go to that man's house," Mary murmured to her sister.

"I know, but we must." Martha blinked hard as she spoke. "I will never leave your side."

Mary wondered if Martha was afraid that she would run away. She wanted to, after all. She knew she couldn't, though. This was her fault. She would face the consequences.

As they reached the house, Mary's thoughts turned on her again. *He is in there. He will hurt you again. He will take you and throw you out into the street like rubbish. And that is surely what you are.*

"I cannot look at him!" Mary cried out. Her legs gave way, and she sank to her knees on the portico at the door. She was shaking and crying. It took both Martha and Lazarus to raise her back to her feet.

Nicodemus took a deep breath and knocked on the door. After a few seconds, a house servant appeared. He looked at the strangers, raised an eyebrow at Lazarus and his sisters, and then focused his attention back on Nicodemus. "Shalom, friends."

"Peace be on this household," Nicodemus replied. "Is your master at home?"

The young man bowed and ushered the group through the door. He gestured to a small room to his right. "The women may wait in here," he said.

Martha and Mary nodded and entered, finding cushions upon which to sit near a small window. The men disappeared into a room beyond a draped curtain.

"I want to leave," Mary said, holding fast to her sister's wrist.

"I know you do. We will leave when it is time. Lazarus must speak with these men."

Mary's veil stuck to her face from the tears she had been unaware of shedding. Martha pulled it back to let her breathe.

"I will be punished, maybe stoned. Nicodemus all but said so." Mary's voice sounded wild in her own ears.

Martha shook her head. "That is not what he said. He came with us to bring reason to Gad and to our brother. He will not allow such things to happen."

Mary pulled at the damp flap of fabric that had covered her face. Her hands shook, and she could smell earth and sweat all around her. "Nobody can stop terrible things from happening. It is all around us. Look at me. Look at you," she said, pulling back the veil over Martha's face. "We are the same now. Both ruined."

Mary saw a look of hate mixed with sadness in Martha's eyes as she repositioned her scarf. They spent the next several minutes in silence.

From the other room, they could hear the men greeting each other. Mary recognized Omar's voice. He sounded happy and welcoming. She heard another man speaking, too. She guessed that he was Omar's father.

A few seconds later the men's conversation grew softer, more serious. Mary and Martha both strained to listen.

Suddenly a maidservant entered, followed by another woman who took a seat near the door. The servant girl brought them each a cup of water, nodding to them as she placed the cups into their hands.

"This is my house," the woman at the door said once the girl had left them. "I am Tirzah. Gad is my husband." She offered a sincere but timid smile.

Martha nodded. "Thank you for allowing us to come in and rest. I am Martha, and this is my sister, Mary. We have traveled from Bethany this morning."

"Yes, I just welcomed your brother."

Martha took a sip of water and tilted her chin to Mary, prompting her to do the same. Mary peered over her cup, watching Tirzah's expression change as she saw Mary's hands trembling.

The woman rose from her cushion and strode to Mary's side. "I heard some of what the men were saying. Your brother accused my son in front of a member of the Sanhedrin."

Mary dropped her cup, spilling water in her lap and splashing her sister. She could no longer control the shaking. She reached out to Martha. "I will die here," she said. "I will die."

Tirzah tilted her head and studied Mary's face. She reached out carefully to touch the scrapes and bruises.

"Then your sister is a liar!" thundered a voice from the other room. All three women jumped in fear. The volume from behind the curtain rose to an unintelligible din.

Tirzah shook her head and rushed out of the room. Mary guessed that she had gone to support her husband and son. "I will die," she moaned again.

The men's conversation quieted, and Martha gave Mary the rest of her water. "Please drink something. It is a long walk home."

"Can you not see? Can you not hear? I will not be going home. I am to die. They all have said it. I am guilty. I should die." Mary swayed forward and back on her knees. Her whole body shook with each syllable.

Martha wrapped her arms around her sister. "Shhh."

Lazarus appeared in the doorway with Nicodemus at his side. "Come, sisters, we shall go home."

Mary felt herself being lifted to her feet. Martha took one side, and Lazarus took the other, and soon they were shuffling her back out to the street. Nicodemus lingered for a few seconds to speak with Gad and then hurried to catch up with them.

Their pace slowed, and Mary was able to walk on her own.

"You warned me not to come," Lazarus said.

Nicodemus shook his head. "I do not blame you for trying. She is your sister. Mary and Martha are all you have left."

"And now I have given them cause." Lazarus coughed. He peered over his shoulder to his sisters. "Oh, what have I done?"

Nicodemus patted his arm. "Do not worry. I warned Gad not to bring this to the council. I reminded him that we have bigger problems to deal with these days and that a woman with scars may garner sympathies with the other members of the Sanhedrin."

As he spoke, the house servant who had greeted them at the door appeared, followed by Tirzah. "My mistress wishes to talk to the women if she may."

Mary stared wide-eyed at the men. Martha nodded. Tirzah approached and took the sisters aside.

Again the woman reached out to touch Mary's battered face. "My son did this to you?" she asked.

Mary could see that she already knew the answer. She nodded.

"Omar is my husband's pride, but he is my disgrace. I am sick at heart over the man he has become." Tirzah's voice rattled with emotion. She held out a small box to Mary.

Mary looked down at the box, but she hadn't the strength to take it. Her hands shook at her sides. Tirzah patted her shoulder and gave the box to Martha. "Take this for your sister. I wish I could offer more, but this is all I have that will not be missed. You see, much to my heartache, Omar is betrothed to another young woman. Their wedding feast is in another month. My other treasures are to go to her, and I have no doubt that she will need them."

Mary cried at the thought of Omar hurting another girl as he had hurt her.

Martha took the box and nodded. "You are a generous woman."

"I am a woman who understands what you face." Tirzah exchanged a glance with Martha that Mary struggled to understand. The older woman leaned over to place a gentle kiss on Mary's forehead. "I would like to visit you at your home sometime."

Martha nodded. "We would welcome you."

"Do not worry about your sister," Tirzah assured Martha. "I will not allow Gad or Omar to bring charges against anyone in your family."

"You are more than generous," Martha repeated as the woman and her servant returned home.

Mary stared at the box in Martha's grasp. "What is it?"

"We will see when we get home," Martha replied. The women walked back to where Lazarus and Nicodemus were talking.

"Thank you, my friend, for trying. I know that having you there to support us helped." Lazarus kissed the man on both cheeks. "I will call on you again soon."

Nicodemus raised his brows and shrugged. "I will do my best to see you. I was not exaggerating about the troubles of the council. A man is stirring up trouble throughout the region. Making all sorts of claims. Turning brother against brother."

Lazarus scowled. "Another zealot?"

"Worse. Some say he is a prophet. A man of God, who is calling himself the King of the Jews." He shook his head. "One like that can push people to revolt. Just the thing Caesar would like to quash. Send our people back to slavery in our own land."

Mary tried to listen to what the men were saying, but the voices in her mind joined with her pounding heartbeat and the afternoon heat to drown out every other sound.

"Stop! Stop!" She tried to scream. Her vision blurred and everything turned a blinding yellow, and then faded to black.

SIX

A flush of shame came over her again. Of course, the gossips were busy talking about her. She had gone mad. She had disgraced her family again.

She began rocking from side to side, holding her arms across her empty stomach. She wanted to disappear.

Martha and Lazarus stood in the doorway, taking a second to see what was wrong. Lazarus went back to the other room, and Martha flew to her side.

"You are finally awake, Mary. Did you have another bad dream?" she asked.

"What is a dream?" Mary said with a cough. "Everything is wrong. Whether I am asleep or awake, everything is bad."

Martha tried to wrap her in her arms. "Shush, now. You have slept for a whole day. You need something to eat. You will feel better with something in your belly."

Mary shook her head. "I do not want food."

"You must eat something. You need your strength," Martha insisted.

"I do not need anything. I will stay in the house and wither away. That requires no strength at all."

Martha blinked at her reply. Mary could see that Martha knew she'd been listening to them.

"*I need you* to help me keep this house from falling apart. *I need you* to stay strong for that." Martha reached for the comb to smooth out Mary's tangles.

"I am sorry to be such an embarrassment to you and Lazarus," Mary whispered.

"You are my precious sister. I am always proud of you," Martha assured her.

"As long as I look right and behave."

Martha stopped combing. "We want only good things for you. People say hurtful things."

"They do. But I think their words hurt you and Lazarus more than me," Mary said.

Martha stood up and frowned at her sister. "People in town, both in Jerusalem and in Bethany, can hurt all of us. Not just with their words."

Mary dropped her gaze to the floor.

"Our brother is doing his best to keep us fed and sheltered." Martha propped her hands on her hips. "The fire stole everything from us. From all of us."

Mary felt herself shudder with a chill. She tried to nod an acknowledgment.

"You were our last hope to regain some standing in our community. You know that. We are attempting to recover from this situation." Martha's voice sounded exhausted. "All we ask is that you try, too."

Mary looked up at her sister and narrowed her gaze. "I have nothing left to offer. I understand that. No man will ever want me for a wife. I will try to do whatever you ask of me, but my mind is filled with terrible thoughts all of the time."

Martha knit her brows and knelt at Mary's side. "What kind of thoughts? I do not know what you mean."

"I hear thoughts in my ears, like ghosts talking to me. They say horrible things."

Martha shook her head. "But that is not real. Just do not listen to those thoughts."

Mary stared at her sister with complete confusion in her eyes. "How is it not real? I hear it as I hear you right now."

Martha sighed, still shaking her head. "You cannot hear them. Not really."

"I can," Mary insisted. "I can!"

Lazarus joined Martha. They each took one of Mary's hands. "Calm down, sister," he said. "We love you."

"But you cannot hear what I hear. I am mad!" Mary struggled to pull her hands free from their grip. Her head ached, and her voice echoed through the whole room.

Martha and Lazarus held her tightly until she stopped struggling. Mary gave up and dropped back to lie across the bed. Her thoughts raced, and the whispers began again. *They will never understand you.*

Her stomach growled loudly enough for Martha and Lazarus to hear.

Martha crossed her arms and stood at the door. "You are hungry, whatever you say. You must eat something."

Lazarus patted his young sister's shoulder. "Everything will be all right, Mary. Martha wants you to eat something. She has made some bread and some olive dip. You must eat."

Mary could barely hear anything Lazarus said. She allowed him to scoop her up and lead her to the table. She dropped onto the mat and stared at the food Martha pushed in front of her. She wanted to eat, but she couldn't stand the sight of the food.

"Why should you eat? You are not worth the cost of the food. You are not worth the time it takes Martha to wipe the table clean." Mary had no idea who was speaking. It might have been the ghosts, her siblings, or herself.

Whoever said it; Martha burst into tears and ran from the house to the garden. Lazarus banged his cup on the table and clutched at the sides of his cloak. He pulled until Mary could hear the seams begin to tear.

"You caused this, Mary!" she heard her own voice say.

"Just eat," Lazarus begged through sobs. "Please just eat something."

Mary picked up her bread and tore it into pieces. She pushed a shred into the olive sauce and then shoved it into her mouth. She barely chewed before she forced herself to swallow. Glaring at her brother, she repeated the process until the bread was gone. Lazarus just shook his head and joined Martha outside.

Mary watched them through the open door. Lazarus wrapped his arm around Martha's shoulder, and she buried her face in his chest. Mary could see Martha's back tremble as she cried. Mary wanted to feel sorry for her. She was sorry, but not for Martha. Not for Lazarus. She was sorry for herself.

Why were they sad? They would never enjoy the wealth their family once had. They would never again be lauded at the temple gates or celebrated in the market. Mary did feel sorry for that, but was it her fault?

"It is your fault," she whispered to herself. "You had to go alone. You had to speak to the men. You did this."

But why is this all my responsibility? Why must this all fall to me? It was not my fault that Martha's husband left her when she was scarred. It was not my fault that Dinah's father retracted his offer to Lazarus. It was not my fault that the crop caught fire and destroyed everything. It was not my fault our parents are dead.

"But you were the last hope for redemption for the family," she hissed. "Lazarus and Martha will go on suffering."

She sat quietly for a moment, watching her siblings mourn in the garden as stars began to light up the black sky. Her heart felt cold.

"What about my suffering?!" she howled.

SEVEN

Mary awoke at home in her bed. Her back ached, and her head pounded. The sky beyond the window was a hazy purple, and Mary couldn't tell if it was early morning or dusk. Her stomach growled.

"Something must be done, but what?" Mary could hear Martha say from the next room.

"What can we do?" Lazarus responded. "How can gossip travel so quickly? I was in Bethany at the market for less than an hour, and I could hear people talking about her. They say she is mad—possessed by a demon."

"Of course, she is not possessed by a demon," Martha defended her. "She is our sister."

Lazarus didn't respond right away. "I know," he finally said, "but you must admit this has changed her."

"Yes," Martha answered. "But that is not her fault."

Mary tried to imagine their faces as she listened to their quiet conversation. She smiled when she realized that theirs were the only voices in her ears. She didn't even care that they were talking about her.

"For a while, we can keep her at home," Lazarus said. "When her bruises are healed, perhaps she will be ready to see others."

Martha clicked her tongue. "The bruises we see are not the most severe injuries she faces."

Mary heard the rattle of a cup on the table. They were eating. The thought prompted her stomach to growl again. She started to stand, but her energy was gone. She struggled just to sit upright in the bed.

"I will take Nicodemus's colt back to Jerusalem tomorrow. Perhaps he can suggest a remedy for Mary," Lazarus said.

Mary tried to remember what happened to her last. She recalled being in Jerusalem, going to Omar's home, seeing Tirzah on the road, and then saying good-bye to Nicodemus. Everything was foggy, but she was sure that she remembered all of that.

An image of a donkey flashed in her mind. She thought she was riding the beast, bumping along the path. It seemed more like a dream. She could hear herself talking, crying, and even screaming. Then she heard a donkey bray from just beyond the window. She remembered that sound, too.

Mary waited until Lazarus had left for Jerusalem and Martha was busy working in the garden before she got up from the bed. She stared at her comb and her head scarf. They meant nothing to her.

She wandered out of the bedroom and into the main room of the tiny house. Everything appeared to be in its place. She noticed the box Tirzah had given her was sitting on the shelf next to the jar of cooking oil.

The ornately carved stone container looked strange in their modest home. The small feet under the box looked like golden eagles' claws. The white-veined alabaster body had been shaped all around, with gold impressed into the etchings. The lid looked like a royal cradle, with a gold loop on either end. It was sealed to the box with some kind of mixture of plaster and wax. Mary wondered what was inside.

What did it matter? She would never know.

Mary turned her back on the room deliberately and marched out the door. She was ready to face Martha's objections or pity, or whatever she might throw. But instead, Mary found that she was alone. Perhaps Martha had gone to fetch water. Mary wasn't sure if she was upset or relieved that Martha wasn't there to stop her.

Mary considered making the trip to the well but then decided against it. *Do not be so stupid, girl.*

Instead, she headed toward Jerusalem. There was a rocky outcropping on the side of the road. Many people had lost their footing there over the years and fallen into the ravine below and died. It was just the place to think about what to do next.

As she walked, a chorus of voices thundered in her mind. *You know what must be done. Martha and Lazarus will be humiliated for a time, but soon they will realize that you have saved them from a lifetime of suffering.*

You do not need to throw yourself off the road. You can live in Jerusalem. Away from Martha and Lazarus. You have all you need to survive. Your bruises are almost healed. Men will pay for you. Your face is still pretty. You can make enough silver to help restore your family's estate.

The road traffic began to increase, both to and from Bethany. Mary did her best to stay on the edge of the path, avoiding eye-contact with anyone. She knew full well that everyone who noticed her stared. Her wild, uncovered hair and rumpled clothing brought plenty of attention. She imagined the whispers of the passers-by which fueled more fiery outbursts within her imagination.

"Live or die. What difference can it make now? Do you think your family will accept the earnings of a prostitute? You should just throw yourself off the road. You should be dead and in Sheol. But to face God naked in torment?" she shrieked.

She looked up for a moment to see a woman pulling her children to the opposite side of her as they passed.

"What does it matter? God has left me to face the world naked." Mary pulled at her dress as if it confined her. "I must decide. To live in humiliation or die in utter darkness."

She had come to the place in the road where she would choose. Ahead in the distance, she could see the gates of Jerusalem. To her north, she could see Gethsemane on the hill. And to her left, she could see death. The narrow valley below looked peaceful. She sat on the rocks to think.

She swallowed hard and realized that she'd had nothing to drink all morning, and a bitter thirst clawed at her throat. She tasted the dirt from the road mixing with a hint of bile. The sun heated her thick black hair like bread baking in an oven. Her heart—her soul—felt dry and empty. The only thing she had left was hate.

"That hate is plenty. It will give you the strength you need," Mary hissed. She looked down at the thorny brush in the deepest part of the ravine below. "You could be down there for months before anyone found you." The idea almost calmed her. "Perhaps you would never be found. Surely the wolves would see to that."

Mary shook her head as she gazed back to the golden city ahead. "But there is an opportunity." She drew a searing breath and stood to face the gates. *Not for one like you. You have no skills. You have no bed to offer. You would be nothing more than a street harlot, begging for a piece of copper or a scrap of bread. You would only bring more shame to your name. You have nothing. You are nothing.*

She sank back to the rock. "Then death is the only answer." She reconciled her mind to the fact. The truth. "There is nothing left. Perhaps I am never found. Lazarus's friends might take pity on him and on Martha. They might offer help to them after losing their poor mad sister without a trace. Who will mourn you, though? No one. No one will mourn. No one will miss you at all."

With the decision made, Mary stood again and took another deep breath. She could feel the flames of Gehenna burning through her lungs. She was halfway there already. The idea of finally silencing the voices gave her a feeling of great peace.

"Yahweh, be with Martha and Lazarus," she whispered.

As she leaned forward over the edge of the rocks, she felt a hand reach out and clasp her arm.

"Dear girl, do not harm yourself," the urgent request came.

Mary turned to see Tirzah and her house servant. They took both her arms and led her away from the side of the road. "What are you thinking, child?"

Mary shook her head. She had no reply. Who could understand?

"I know you are desperate," Tirzah said with a shimmer in her eyes. "Do not allow what happened to you in one day to destroy your whole life."

Mary pressed her lips into a thin, tense line. She didn't want to speak, but she felt the words forming. She shook her head violently, but the thoughts poured out.

"I am destroyed. There is no life left in me, can you not see this? My thoughts are broken. My mind is as battered as my body."

Tirzah held Mary's face in her hands. "Your body is heal-ing. Look." She took Mary's hands and stretched her fore-arms between them. "Your mind can heal, too."

"It never will," Mary moaned. "I will never be the same."

Tirzah blinked. "Of course, you will not be the same. No person could remain untouched after such a trauma. You cannot hold yourself to that standard."

Mary bit down on her bottom lip until she drew blood. Tirzah gestured to her servant who handed her a skin of water.

"Drink this," Tirzah ordered. "Drink slowly, but drink as much as you like."

Mary wanted to resist, but she couldn't help but drink.

The water felt cold in her over-heated body, and she could trace its path down her throat to her stomach.

Tirzah motioned to her servant again, and the young man took Mary's arm.

"We shall take you home," she announced. "My man and I will stay at your house tonight, and I will speak with your brother and sister. Do you understand me?"

Mary nodded. *More humiliation.*

The voices continued to rant as they walked home, though Mary managed to keep them inside as much as she could. A few outbursts brought the attention of other travelers, but Tirzah seemed to ignore them. Instead, she glared until the strangers looked to their own business.

At the path leading to her home, Mary froze in the middle of the road. Tirzah halted her servant. "Is this the way?" she asked Mary.

"I cannot go back," Mary replied. A whole chorus screamed through her thoughts, and her feeble voice seemed an inadequate response.

"You can," Tirzah said. "I will not tell them what you were about to do back there. That is for you alone. But they need to see you again."

Mary's heart pounded more loudly with every step. As they approached, Lazarus and Martha came running to meet them. Mary kept her gaze on the path.

She felt as though she was being dragged inside by a mob. She tried to pull away from their grasp, but her body was too weak. Weak and helpless. Helpless and hopeless.

She tried to cry. She heaved to the point of retching, but her body was depleted. She fell in a heap on the floor just inside the house. The dirt and stone felt cool to her skin, and suddenly she was aware of how hot her hair was on her neck.

Lazarus and Martha picked up their sister and carried her to her bed.

"She needs something to eat and drink," Tirzah said. Her voice sounded motherly, and Martha hurried to prepare some nourishment.

"Where did you find her?" Lazarus asked. Mary could see the worry lines starting to relax in his face.

"She was on the road to Jerusalem," Tirzah answered.

Lazarus sighed. "She must have been looking for me," he said. "I was returning something to a friend this morning."

The older woman pushed a weary smile onto her lips and dipped her chin in acknowledgment. "She is weak."

Martha brought in a tray of food. It was enough for everyone, and Mary wondered if her brother and sister had skipped their meals to search for her.

As they all ate, Mary was aware that she was the focus of the others. Lazarus offered a blessing, and Martha cleared the remains of the meal, but everyone watched what Mary would do next.

She was a caged animal. She wanted to run away. Far away. *Not just to Jerusalem. People know you there. You must leave entirely.*

She wrapped her arms across her stomach and tucked her chin to her chest. *Where was far enough?*

Tirzah reached out and took Martha's hand. "Perhaps we should let her rest," she suggested.

And with that, Mary was alone. She stretched out on the

bed and rolled over to face the wall. She could not see the others, but she could hear them.

"Has she been like this since you brought her to Jerusalem?" Tirzah asked.

"She seems to get worse as time passes," Martha responded.

Lazarus quickly interjected, "Perhaps not worse, but not better."

"It is worse," Martha said.

Tirzah's voice sounded sure and controlled. "I have heard of a man that may be able to help her."

"Who?" Martha and Lazarus asked together.

"He is called Jesus of Nazareth. He has many followers. He teaches in the temple courts sometimes. Some call him rabbi. Some say he can heal. I have not heard him speak, but I have heard of his work."

"Nicodemus said he was causing trouble," Lazarus said.

Mary heard a strange voice. She wasn't sure if it was one of her voices at first, but soon she realized it was Tirzah's servant.

"I have heard him teach. He is surely a great prophet. I witnessed with my own eyes a miracle from his hand. There was a man, lame for years. I have seen him in the same place begging in the market. Jesus told him to rise and walk. Just as one might ask the price of fish, he said, 'Rise and walk.'" The servant paused for a second. "And the beggar stood up. He not only walked but began to jump and dance. I could see that his legs were strong. They were changed before my own eyes."

"How can this be true?" Lazarus asked.

Martha interrupted. "He could have been able to walk before, just too lazy to work."

"No, mistress," the servant insisted. "I tell you what I saw was true."

Tirzah's voice remained calm. "I believe him. Josiah has not lied to me before. And why would he lie about this now?"

"Why indeed?" Lazarus said. "But there are men all over who claim to heal. They do tricks for money. For entertainment."

"I tell you," Josiah insisted. "I saw the muscles in his legs grow strong as I watched. The expression on the healed man's face was something to behold. From pain and helplessness to joy." Josiah almost laughed. "He took my hand and danced."

Mary's thoughts roared to drown out the conversation in the other room. *You cannot hope for a cure for your madness. This is no disease. This is who you are now. You know you must die.*

She clutched at the sides of her head. "Stop!" she screamed. "I know I must die!"

Lazarus was at her side before she realized she was out of bed. His arms surrounded her and held fast as she reached out to the door.

"I must go!" she cried. "You will all be better without me." Tears finally came, and with them, her body surrendered to exhaustion. She collapsed into a thick darkness that held no hope for rest.

EIGHT

Mary woke from her nightmares to a bustling household. Josiah was outside preparing water skins while Martha and Tirzah made breakfast. Mary could smell bread baking, and her stomach growled.

Martha was soon at her side helping her bathe and dress for the day. Mary wasn't sure of the plan, but she could see that there was certainly something about to happen.

Lazarus walked through the door as Mary sat beside Tirzah on a cushion at the table. "Josiah is packing our things onto the donkey. Once we have all eaten, we can go."

Martha reached out for Mary's hand. "We are going to take a little trip to see someone today. He may be able to help you."

Mary stared at the burn scars running from Martha's wrist to her jaw. Though they had healed considerably in two years, they still looked terrible. Her other arm was smooth and healthy, but the burnt arm looked withered. A dark brown leather had formed where red blisters had been. Mary thought that even if someone could help her, however impossible that seemed, she would remain scarred like Martha. Only her scars would be invisible to everyone else.

Do not imagine there is any healing for you. "Your scars will never heal!" Mary screeched.

Martha looked shocked, and Mary knew that Martha thought she was talking about the burns. Martha pulled back her arm and turned away.

Tirzah took a firm grasp of Mary's hand. "Quiet." She looked at the others. "Come and sit here. She needs you, no matter how she pushes you away."

Mary watched as Lazarus and Mary found their places at the table. They all ate breakfast in a tense silence. Mary was glad for the quiet. She knew it would not last, but she was grateful for the moment.

When the food was gone, and the house straightened, they were ready to go.

Lazarus helped Mary onto the donkey, and the others walked on either side. Their small troupe traveled up the road to Jerusalem and entered the gates at noon. Tirzah had Josiah run ahead to her home and prepare lunch for them all. She assured Lazarus that Gad and Omar had both gone for a short trip north to Damascus. The house would be at her command.

When they reached the door, Josiah greeted them and instructed another servant to wash their feet. He led them to a table set with fresh fruit and cheeses. Two maidservants attended the meal until everyone was satisfied.

Mary's head was dizzy again. She felt the urge to run

away again, but she knew it was hopeless. *Everything was hopeless.* She tried to listen as the others spoke in nervous tones.

"What if he cannot help her?" Lazarus asked. "If I am seen with him, I may bring more trouble to our name. Nicodemus said he stirred trouble."

Martha clicked her tongue. "If you feel you should not go, then stay here. Tirzah has already offered to take Mary without us."

Mary noticed that Martha said, "without us," implying that she wouldn't go if Lazarus didn't.

Everyone is afraid of you.

"No, I will go," he replied. "I just hope not to make matters worse."

"What is worse than this?" Mary blurted.

Tirzah turned sharply to face her. "There are many, many things worse than this, child. It may not seem so now. I hope this is the very worst thing you face in your life, but the longer you live, the more trouble you will see. That is life."

Mary blinked at the mild scolding. She knew that Tirzah pitied her, but apparently she had no intention of commiserating with her.

Martha knit her brows and frowned at Tirzah. "We cannot be too harsh."

"I am not harsh at all," the older woman said. "You have seen pain. More than your fair share. You know that she needs you, but she is no longer a child. We should not treat her as one."

Josiah entered and nodded to his mistress. He turned to face Lazarus and waited for permission to speak.

"Go ahead," Lazarus said.

"The man, Jesus of Nazareth, has been seen outside of the Temple. A group of people is following him. If we hurry, we can see him." Josiah barely waited for a response before helping Mary to her feet.

The others quickly followed, and the group was soon ready to go.

Martha took Mary's hand as they went back into the sunlight. "We are going to see a teacher. We will see if he can help you."

Lazarus raised his eyes to the sky. "Yahweh, help us all."

Tirzah nodded to Mary. "Just hold onto hope a little longer, my dear girl."

Fear gripped Mary more severely than she had felt before. She didn't want to see anyone. Least of all another man. What could a man do for her? All she could think about was what a man had already done to her. She was broken. Beyond repair. Broken in every way. *Run. Run away now. You must escape. There is no hope for you.*

CHAPTER

NINE

Mary's eyes grew increasingly wider as they approached the crowd. A sea of people stretched out before her, and all around she could hear the name 'Jesus' being whispered from one person to another. She grew anxious at the thought of being brought before someone for examination.

He cannot help you. He will expose your shame to the whole city and mock you in front of all of these people. Her stomach twisted in knots and she could hardly keep pace with the others.

Lazarus led the small group, with Tirzah close behind. Martha and Mary were hemmed in by Josiah. They all pushed deeper into the crowd, and Mary's fears chilled her body to the core.

If you could break free from Martha's grip, you could easily get lost in this crowd of people. It would be a simple enough task. Then you could run away and hide. They could not search for you until the people dispersed. You could be out of Jerusalem by then.

Martha must have sensed Mary's thoughts of flight because as her grip on Mary's hand grew tighter by the second.

Martha pulled her along. "Come, sister. The crowd is moving this way. Jesus of Nazareth must be close."

"I do not want to see him," Mary begged. "No one can help me!"

Martha shook her head. "How can you think this? How can you know this?"

"Everyone says that I am beyond hope." Mary could hear the voices screaming in her ears. They were the only thing louder than the beating of her heart.

"No one is beyond hope," Tirzah answered. "Certainly not you, child."

Mary tried to draw a deep breath, but the people pressed too closely on every side. There was not enough air for everyone. Not enough air for Mary to breathe. She struggled to pull her hand free again, but Martha held firm. Mary pressed her left hand to her chest. She felt as though her heart was going to explode. She gasped for breath again, but all she could do was cough.

"Help! Stop!" she cried out.

Martha kept pulling, but Lazarus turned to face his sisters.

"What is it, Mary?" he asked.

"I cannot. I cannot breathe, please, I must rest."

Lazarus and Tirzah exchanged glances and nodded to Martha. "A minute," Lazarus agreed.

As soon as they stopped, Mary bent at the waist and ducked her head to her chest. She pushed hard and in an instant, was loose from Martha's grasp. She began to run as fast as she could. People were everywhere, blocking her path in every direction. Within seconds, Josiah had clasped his hands around both her arms, just above the elbows.

"Be gentle with her," Tirzah admonished. "She is scared enough."

Mary burst into tears. "I do not want to see Jesus," she cried.

"But Mary," Martha said, struggling not to cry. "You want to be healed, do you not?"

Mary's chest heaved as she began to breathe too quickly. Her thoughts raced from the image of a man dressed in the blue robes of a high priest towering over her crumpled body and proclaiming guilt, to a vision of an ancient healer declaring that there was no cure for her. Either way, both images ended with her execution.

She huddled on the ground with her arms wrapped around her knees. "Please do not make me go any farther."

Martha looked at Lazarus and Tirzah with sad eyes. She still held Mary's hand, but now she was sitting beside her on the ground. Mary was holding Martha's hand as tightly as Martha held hers.

Tirzah shook her head. "You may rest for a minute, but I believe that you really must see him," she said.

As Mary continued to weep, she could hear a strange murmur in the crowd. People were shifting their direction around them. Her heart pounded even more loudly than before.

She could hear Lazarus speaking to someone. "Rabbi, my

sister is greatly troubled with an anxious spirit. We have brought her to you for a blessing."

Mary looked up, and for a moment, the bright sun blinded her vision. A second later a man's silhouette blocked the sunlight as he stood over her. Her head screamed for her to run, but she was frozen in place.

The man was neither intimidating nor dressed in fine robes. He looked like any other man in the crowd around them. He knelt at Mary's side and looked into her eyes.

He took her hand from Martha and moved his lips without making a sound. He then nodded and said, "Mary, you have seen such sadness in your time, you and your family. But the spirit within you has gone now, and you are clean. You belong to my Father, and you are made whole."

Mary's tears dried, and the screaming in her head vanished. She could suddenly breathe without struggling. A warmth deeper than the sun poured over her, and she real- ized that she was smiling. Not just a timid grin, but a full- face from-the-heart smile.

"Thank you," she said.

She allowed Jesus to gently pull her to her feet again, and Martha stood at her side.

Lazarus continued, "If you would be willing to help her. . ."

Jesus smiled at him. "I have."

"Is there something we should do? Or something we should give her?" Lazarus asked, still unaware of what had taken place before his own eyes.

"Your sister is healed," Jesus said. "You may take her home if you wish."

"What?" Lazarus and Martha asked at the same time.

Mary almost laughed. "I am well. He healed me. The voices are gone."

Tirzah raised her hands to the sky. "Praise Yahweh," she said. She turned to Lazarus. "Look at her. You can see it in her eyes. Jesus healed her."

Mary nodded to the others. "Thank you."

Jesus smiled at Mary and then at Lazarus. "You brought your sister to see me from Bethany. I travel through there often. I will see you again. Take your sisters home."

Mary watched as Jesus walked a short distance to speak to a woman carrying a baby in her arms. She saw him reach out and touch the baby's tiny fist and laugh.

Tirzah released a long sigh of relief. "We should go. You all will eat supper with me before you depart."

Mary shook her head. "May we please stay? I want to see what else Jesus will do?"

Lazarus knit his brows and frowned. "You are tired. Another day."

She wanted to argue, to tell him that she wasn't tired anymore. She wanted to tell all of them that she felt like flying. For the first time since her parents died, she felt whole. She knew that she would see Jesus again.

As they walked back to Tirzah's home, Mary felt her smile growing bigger. Her thoughts still raced, but they were no longer filled with troubles or fears. No more taunting screams or wicked accusations. She thought of what she might be able to do or say to make others understand the gift that this man had given to her.

He gave her worth. He gave her purpose.

"Martha, we should get the house ready for Jesus to visit."

Martha and Lazarus stared at her as if she spoke another language.

Tirzah laughed as she led them in to have their feet washed. "He is certainly a great healer," she said.

Josiah nodded as he instructed the servants with the wash basins and towels. "I have seen his miracles before. I believe he is more than a healer. He is from God."

Mary nodded. "I know that to be true. My mind was clouded, my head crowded with pain and fear. And when he touched me, that all disappeared."

"But how?" Martha asked. "I did not hear him speak at all. The crowd was too thick. Too loud."

Mary shrugged. "I cannot tell how he healed me. I cannot say from where the voices came or where they went. I can only say that they are indeed gone."

They all sat down to supper. Lazarus gave the traditional meal blessing and added praise to Yahweh for sending Jesus to heal Mary. After dinner, Lazarus thanked Tirzah. Martha and Mary hugged her and invited her to visit soon.

Tirzah had Josiah bring their donkey to them at the street. It was packed with several bags of household items and foods.

Lazarus started to object. "We are not beggars. You are too generous."

Tirzah shook her head. "These are not only for you. When Jesus comes to your house, he will have many with him. You will need this extra to care for him."

Lazarus shook his head and shrugged. He knew better

than to argue. "Thank you for all you have done for my sister."

As they took the Jericho Road back home, Mary was grateful for the longer days of sunlight. She let the heat shower her face, and she said prayer after prayer of thanksgiving. They reached the path to her house just as the sun was going down behind them.

Mary looked at their home with renewed eyes. The little two-room storehouse now seemed fresh and full of hope. "Tomorrow I will find Ema's loom and repair it. I think I would like to weave again."

Martha smiled. "That would be pleasant for you."

Lazarus led the donkey to the door and began to unpack. "Tirzah is too generous. We should go through all this tomorrow. I think I will stay home for a few days to make sure that you are both well."

Mary hugged her brother's neck and laughed. "I am well. Martha is well. Everything is much better. Tomorrow we will go through Tirzah's gifts, and you shall go back to work. You have spent too much time worrying about me already."

They all washed and went to their beds. Mary prayed for God's peace to cover their house and to follow her brother throughout the week. As she began to drift off to sleep, she could still see Jesus' silhouette standing over her. Calm covered her like a blanket.

She finally closed her eyes without fear of sleep.

CHAPTER

TEN

"I need to get back to Jeb's place," Lazarus announced after breakfast. "Will you be all right without me here?" he asked.

As Mary did her morning chores, she had listened to Martha and Lazarus weigh the benefits and drawbacks of his absence. She knew the decision had already been made, but she was happy to have the opportunity to offer her opinion. "We will manage without you." She kissed her brother on his cheek.

"I shall return for Shabbat, and then be another week if he needs me."

Martha smiled and nodded. "Mary wants to work on Ema's loom. I think we can repair it today, and then perhaps find some wool. We will be busy enough here."

"Good," Lazarus said. "If anything happens, send word right away."

Both sisters nodded, and soon they wished him well and

watched as he disappeared over the hill toward their neighbor's home.

Mary drew a deep, refreshing breath. "Oh, Martha, I wish I could tell you how much better I feel. When Jesus spoke my name, I still do not know how he knew my name, but his voice was calm and sure."

"I can see that you are better. It is more than obvious. But he did not seem to do anything. He barely spoke to you at all. Perhaps a minute, but certainly not longer." Martha twisted her lips. Mary had seen that fretful look before.

"To say he only spoke for a minute, I suppose it is true. It seemed much longer to me. The crowd was pressing all around us, but when he touched my hand, I could see or hear no one but him." Mary patted her sister's shoulder. "We should look for the loom."

They found the wooden frame without too much trouble and then spent another hour repairing the corner pieces that kept everything tight. Martha finished her chores while Mary searched through Ema's salvaged things for some wool. There wasn't enough to complete any large project, but there was plenty of thin yarn to run the vertical warp threads over the loom, even fully extended.

"Maybe we can go to the market in Bethany later this week for more wool. Or I can use the remnants we have to make something. It might not be pretty, but it would be good to practice." Mary perused the small bundles of yarn. "There is no way to make a real pattern with these, but a coverlet with a little of everything. That would be all right, I think."

"Of course. That would be suitable." Martha finished her work and joined Mary at the loom. She helped secure the threads across the frame and picked up the shuttle for examination. "We should clean this, and maybe use some wax to keep it smooth. Mother always kept her tools in such lovely condition."

Martha turned to face her sister. Mary smiled and hugged Martha's shoulder. "She would be proud of us, you know."

Martha raised her eyebrows as if she never expected to hear Mary say those words. "She would. She would be very proud of you."

Mary shook her head. "She would be proud of all three of us."

A rap on the door startled them both. Mary hopped to her feet and peered out the window. She nodded for Martha to open the door.

"Shalom." Josiah greeted them with a slight bow.

Martha invited him inside. Mary noticed four men behind him. They tended a cart and donkey in the yard.

"May we offer you some water?" Martha said, gesturing to the cushions around the table.

Josiah stepped through the door but did not sit. "My mistress sent us to help prepare your house for receiving guests."

Martha fixed a gracious smile on her face. "Your mistress has already been too kind."

"She would not allow us to return without completing the task she has set."

Mary smiled, too. "What task is this?"

Josiah bowed again. "We are to add a portico and a room over your house."

"What?" Martha said with a gasp.

"It will not take long. We are skilled, and we have all that we need," Josiah explained.

Martha shook her head. "That is too much. Your mistress is too kind."

"Forgive me," Josiah said. "She insisted. We will not be in your way."

Mary laughed. "She insisted?"

Josiah smiled. "Her words were, 'Please allow me the gift of showing favor to a family whom God himself favors.'" Josiah paused. "Her words."

Martha blinked. Mary took a deep breath and nudged her sister. "We would be honored to receive her blessing."

Martha raised her hands, palms up, as if in surrender. "But you must allow us to bring you something to eat before you begin."

Josiah nodded. "We will be honored to receive your blessings."

Mary watched as Josiah walked back to the cart to instruct the men for the building project. "What do you think Lazarus will say when he returns?" she asked.

Martha shrugged. "Oh, who can say how he will react?"

Mary laughed as they worked together to make a quick lentil stew and bread. When the men finished their lunch, they went right back to laying out beams from the cart. In a few hours, the noise from the hammers became routine to Mary.

Martha gathered a few things from the garden and returned with a wild look in her eyes.

"What is wrong?" Mary asked.

"Nothing. But will you go with me to the market? I need to pick up some more salt and other spices, and perhaps we can find your wool."

Mary nodded and picked up their shopping basket. "You look strange, Martha. Are you sure nothing is wrong?"

Martha chuckled. "I think you will be surprised when you see how our house has already changed."

Mary followed her sister outside and looked back at the house. A row of beams stood guard across the front of the little mud brick house and soared up to create another story above. Josiah's men were more than doubling the size of their home. Mary's mouth hung open as she stared in wonder.

"Is there anything you need, mistress?" Josiah asked.

"No," Martha answered through a mist of pleasant bewilderment. "We are going to Bethany for a few things. We will be back soon."

Josiah whistled to one of his men, and they spoke for a few seconds. Afterward, he took a quick drink of water and gestured to Martha. "I will accompany you."

Mary saw that Martha started to resist, but then she must have decided that it would be useless to argue. The three of them began the short walk into the small village.

"You are a good servant to Tirzah," Mary said to Josiah.

"She is a good woman," he replied. "She likes you both very much."

Martha's expression seemed to change. "She need not feel as though she owes our family." A hint of a frown pulled at the corners of her lips.

Josiah must have noticed as well. "And you should not feel

that this is her pity. She is happy to have friends with whom she can share. In Jerusalem, she spends most of her days alone."

Mary understood now how loneliness felt. Even as the voices had crowded her thoughts, she remembered the despair of feeling that no one else was there for her. That nobody else could possibly understand or care.

"We will visit," she chirped.

Martha and Josiah both shot a warning glance.

Mary quickly realized her mistake. Of course, they could not visit Tirzah in her home again. If Gad or Omar was there, if friends or neighbors told them, how dreadful the consequences would be for their friend.

"She can visit us here," Mary said. She wished she could hug Tirzah at that very moment. "She can visit whenever it is convenient for her."

Josiah and Martha nodded. Mary sighed. Her heart had been cleaned of the trouble. She wished everyone could experience the same thing.

The market bustled with crowds buying food, linens, and all sorts of goods. Martha found the spices she needed without too much haggling. Mary shopped for wool. She found several bundles that she liked and finally settled on a spool of soft, blue yarn. Josiah found a large water jar and purchased it with his own silver.

Mary noticed several women whispering and gesturing to her, but she decided not to take it personally. Instead, she offered her neighbors a gentle smile and a sincere, "Shalom." After that, the whispers seemed to subside.

Martha stopped at one last booth to pick up some salted

fish, and then they were ready to return home. Josiah helped carry anything that didn't fit into the basket, and soon they were on their way.

"I hope it will not be too late for you and your men," Martha said, as they turned onto the path to their house.

"My men and I will sleep at your well, with your permission," Josiah said.

"You are not afraid of wild animals?" Mary asked. She grinned at the man, knowing that animals were not the primary concern of those who slept outside. Robbers were often more dangerous than animals anywhere along the Jericho Road.

"We have a tent. And we can defend ourselves if need be."

Mary appreciated Josiah's answer though Martha appeared troubled.

"The well. . ." she began but stopped.

Josiah nodded. "Is close enough if you need us, but far enough away to prevent talk of impropriety."

Martha nodded again. "Very well."

As they reached the house, Martha froze in her tracks. Mary almost bumped into the back of her. Josiah smiled at their reactions.

Mary looked up to see their house had grown. Considerably. Though the roof was not finished, and the mud bricks were yet to be placed, the framing of the second floor and the portico was complete.

"Lazarus will think he has come to the wrong house," Martha said.

"This is now bigger than our old house," Mary exclaimed.

"The perfect house for receiving the Messiah," Josiah finished.

"The Messiah?" Martha asked.

"That is who my mistress says Jesus is."

Mary smiled, and instantly she knew. Her heart thumped in her chest. "Yes," she said. "Of course, he is the Messiah. He must be."

CHAPTER

ELEVEN

"Stop this foolishness. For a week now, you've been saying that he is the Messiah," Martha said again. "Talk like that is blasphemous."

Mary shrugged and continued weaving at her loom. Her blanket was nearly finished. "How could anyone do the things he does if he is not from God?"

"I am not saying that Jesus is not from God. A prophet, a messenger maybe, but that does not mean he is the Messiah."

Mary sighed. She knew that Martha was too practical to consider or to hope for such a thing. After all, the Messiah would change everything in their lives. Everything in the world. But Mary also knew that kind of change had already happened to her.

Martha continued. "What have we done to deserve the Messiah's arrival?"

Mary listened but didn't respond. She imagined that

Martha was talking just to cover the noise of the construction still going on all around them.

"Mary, we cannot just lightly call a man 'Messiah' without knowing more about him." Martha was cleaning her cookware, preparing for Shabbat supper. "There is still much for our people to do before this world is ready for the Messiah. Still too much evil. Too much greed. Too much hurt."

Mary nodded, but it was more automatic than agreement. "What if that is the Messiah's purpose?"

"To what?" Martha asked.

"I do not know exactly, but if he is to be a Savior, then what will he save us from, if not ourselves?" Mary hadn't planned the question, but somehow it spilled out anyway.

Martha sighed. "I believe the rabbis and priests are better suited to answer these questions than us. I expect they have more educated ideas about if and when the Messiah will come."

Mary grimaced. She wanted to respond, but how? She didn't mean to argue, and Martha was almost always right about such things. Everything she had said made perfect sense. How could Mary dispute that?

Martha seemed to take Mary's lack of reply as a good place to end the conversation. "We should be more worried about what our brother will say when he arrives." Martha glanced out the door. "I expect that he will come soon."

Josiah knocked at the door, which was already open, and waited for Martha to look up.

"Yes, Josiah?"

"We are just finishing our work for the morning, and

then we will go back to Jerusalem. Our mistress will need our help in preparing for the supper tonight." Josiah nodded to Mary. "When the Sabbath is over we will return to finish your house."

Martha smiled. "Just so. And you must thank your mistress for us, and offer our blessings on her household."

Josiah lowered his brow and glanced over at Mary again. "On her *household*?" he asked.

Mary sat up straight and replied. "Yes, Josiah. On her whole household." She still felt upset when she thought about Omar and even Gad, but Mary indeed wished only peace for Tirzah. How could that ever happen without the entire family receiving a blessing?

"Thank you," he said with a deep bow of respect.

In another hour, Josiah and his men had cleaned up the site, packed their cart, and taken the road back to Jerusalem. Before they left, they brought Mary and Martha two filled water jars to save them the trip.

Soon after, the sisters watched Lazarus return from his week of work at Jeb's place. Mary could see a bright look of excitement in his eyes as he approached the house.

"What has happened here?" he exclaimed when he saw the house. "I thought my news was big."

"Tirzah sent Josiah and his men to make some improvements," Mary said as she threw her arms around her brother's neck. "What do you think?"

Lazarus stood in front of the house and stared for several seconds. "It is too much. We cannot. It is too much."

"That is exactly what I told them," Martha explained, "but Josiah said that Tirzah insisted."

Mary nodded. "But you said that you have news?" She looped her arm around her brother's elbow and led him inside.

He sat on the bench at the door and Martha began washing his feet while Mary pulled away his dusty cloak.

"Yes, tell us your news," Martha said.

Lazarus raised his brow and relaxed with a sigh. "Jeb and I have struck a bargain. His crop of wheat was good last year. So good that he had more grain than he could sell at market or sow in his own fields. At first, he asked if he might sell some to me, but I told him that I had no way to pay him for it."

"That is a shame," Martha said. "Our land is fertile this year."

"Yes, that is what he said. Then he asked if he could lease our fields for planting. He will sow the seed, we will help tend it, and then we can divide the profits of the harvest fairly." Lazarus spread a satisfied smile on his face. "His men will begin planting late next week."

Mary and Martha leaped with excitement and hugged each other and then their brother.

"What wonderful news!" Martha said.

"Yes, but there is much to do to prepare." Lazarus motioned to the clean house around him. "I see that you have already begun the preparations. I will need to hire a man to help me clear the fields of rocks before the plow can turn the dirt. And now we have a place to keep him."

"We will worry about all of that after the Sabbath," Martha said. "The sun is starting its descent, and we have much to do before sunset."

Mary helped Lazarus unpack his things before joining Martha to help with the cooking.

"Things are changing, Martha," she said as she placed the platter of food on the table.

Martha smiled and nodded. Mary noticed that Martha stared at the scars on her arm as she poured the cups of watered wine. "Yes, things are changing sister," Martha said. "But change is not always for the better."

CHAPTER

TWELVE

The next week was busy with lots of work on the house and in the field. Lazarus hired a man to help clear the land for planting, and Josiah brought two more workers to help finish the walls and roof of the second floor and portico. Mary and Martha bustled about with projects inside the expanding home and in the garden as well.

Josiah and his crew finished on the same day that Jeb's men began planting. "We will go back to Jerusalem in the morning," he said to Martha. "And my mistress will want to visit you next week. Is there anything we might bring with us when we come back?"

Mary and Martha both shrugged. "You have already done too much," Martha replied.

"Seeing Tirzah will be more than enough," Mary said.

Josiah bowed low and excused himself for the evening.

Martha and Mary began setting the supper table as Lazarus and the new hand returned.

"Asa, join us for the evening meal," Lazarus said, gesturing to a seat cushion.

Mary washed the men's feet and followed them to the table. She poured out their cups of wine and helped Martha bring the rest of the food.

"I have heard of this man, Jesus of Nazareth," Asa said, apparently continuing a previous conversation.

"Yes? And what do you hear?" Lazarus asked.

"He is a smart man, not just smart, but clever, too. He cannot be called a fool by anyone. I have heard rabbis question him, and he always has a thoughtful response, even when their intention is to trip him. He shares meals with the rich and the poor alike, and can hold a conversation with just about anyone."

Mary listened intently. She wanted to hear everything about Jesus. As soon as Martha was ready, the women joined the men at the table.

Asa nodded to the sisters as they sat. "He even speaks with women."

Mary nodded. She wanted to tell Asa about her experience but didn't intend to stop his story.

"I had gone out to hear a man at the Jordan River. They call him 'the Baptizer.' He was the first to speak of Jesus. He told the crowds that they should prepare for Jesus. That they should be ready to follow him. Peculiar. Having droves of people hanging on your every word, and then telling them to follow someone else." Asa tilted his head, shrugged, and then began his meal.

Lazarus agreed. "Not typical at all."

Mary couldn't stand it for another second longer. "Did you see Jesus perform a miracle?"

Everyone turned toward Mary. Martha looked like she wanted to glare, but Mary guessed that she wished to know the answer, too.

Asa smiled. "I did, in fact. A blind man was brought to him. Jesus spoke to him for a minute. Asked a few questions, I suppose. Then Jesus picked up a handful of dirt and spit into it. Mixed it into a mud paste and put it over the man's eyes."

Mary realized that she was up on her knees, leaning over the table in anticipation. She took a quick breath and sat back on her cushion.

Asa continued. "After a few more questions, the man wiped the mud from his eyes, and he could see. I would never have believed it if I had not been there myself."

"I believe it," Mary said. She knew what Jesus had done for her, and she was thrilled that others were seeing Jesus' power, too.

"There is more," Asa said. He paused for a moment to be sure that the others wanted to hear more. Lazarus nodded, and the man went on. "Hundreds of people gather around him wherever he goes. He has a small group of helpers who manage the crowds. People come from everywhere to have him bless their children, heal their ailments, and to hear his stories."

"Stories?" Mary asked.

"Oh yes, he tells all sorts of stories. He talks about fathers and sons, about lost treasures, about kingdoms, about gardens. His knowledge seems endless." Asa interrupted his account to eat a few more bites. "He can talk to one man about a harvest, and then talk to another about the scriptures. He can speak about mending clothes as easily as he talks of wineskins."

Lazarus took a sip of his watered wine. "I should like to hear him talk sometime."

Asa gestured to the west. "You can if you like. He was heading to the Sea of Galilee, I believe I heard. Just a few days' travel from here."

Mary almost leaped from her seat. "Oh Lazarus, may we go? Please?"

Lazarus lowered his brow and twisted his lips as if that helped him to consider the question. He looked at Martha, who also seemed eager for his answer.

"Let me think about it for a while. There is much to do here. We all have a busy week ahead. And you do not yet know when Tirzah will visit."

Martha nodded. "He is right, Mary. What if Tirzah arrived, and we were nowhere to be found?"

Mary scowled. "If anyone understood, it would be Tirzah," Mary murmured, the words wrapped in a sigh.

"We will see," Lazarus said, finishing the conversation.

Mary knew that nothing could be gained by pushing the matter further. She nodded and finished the rest of her meal in quiet thought.

When supper was over and all the chores finished, Mary went out to the portico to enjoy the cool of the evening. She looked up at the stars and breathed in the stillness.

"Are you the Messiah?" she whispered. "You are certainly

a great man, but are you the Deliverer that my father spoke about when I was a child?"

Mary was almost surprised when she heard no response. No voices in her head. No rustling in the wind. No echoes from the hills. Just quiet.

Martha joined her and nudged her elbow. "You should come in and get ready to sleep."

"Do you really believe that Jesus is just a messenger?" Mary asked her older sister.

"Mary, I do not know who or what he is. I would like to see him again so that I could thank him for helping you." She wrapped her arm around Mary's shoulder. "You certainly seem much better."

"Oh, Martha," Mary said, leaning her head back against her sister's arm. "I wish you could feel the difference in my heart and in my mind. It is as though a shroud has been lifted from me. But it is more than that. I feel new." Mary looked around the portico and shrugged. "We should have a better bench for out here. More than this stool."

Martha laughed. "Yes, we should see about that."

Mary circled her arms around Martha's waist. "I know that I am still damaged in the eyes of others. I may never have a husband. I may never have children. Just the thought makes me sad. But Jesus looked at me. He spoke my name and said that I was clean. He knew what had happened to me without me telling him. But he chose to see past that."

Mary looked up and saw a shimmer in Martha's eyes.

"Please do not be sad for me," Mary insisted.

"I am not sad. Well, of course, I am a little sad. But the

way you speak. Your experience is beautiful. I am happy that he saw you as I do."

"The same way you see me?" Mary asked.

"Yes. He saw your heart."

Mary squeezed her. "I wish you could see my heart now," she said.

Martha placed a kiss on Mary's forehead. "I can."

"Then you know how much I want to go the Sea. I want to see and to hear Jesus speak." Mary made her eyes big and pitiful as she looked up at Martha. "Just one more time?"

Martha shook her head. "I will talk to Lazarus, but I will not pester him, and neither shall you."

"I promise," Mary replied.

"You should get some rest tonight. If I am able to convince him, I want you to be alert for the trip to Galilee." Martha slipped out of Mary's embrace and started inside.

"I will be right in," Mary assured her. "I would like to stay a moment longer to pray."

Martha nodded and went inside.

Mary stepped out into the garden and spread her hands up in front of her. She lifted her chin to the sky again. "Yahweh, God, and King of the universe," she began. "Your ways are perfect and holy. Your words are just. Your love never ends. I pray for your peace to rest on this house and on Tirzah's household."

She swallowed hard as she thought of her friend living in the same house as the man who had hurt her. She clutched her hands together. "Lord God Almighty, I ask that you bring hope to Tirzah." She stopped. No more words came. She had a full heart, but none of the words in her mind seemed to fit.

Mary studied the stars for another minute, hoping for inspiration, but her prayer had ended. She drew one last breath of evening air, and then went inside to her bed. She couldn't say exactly what she was feeling, but she knew that tomorrow would bring a new beginning.

CHAPTER

THIRTEEN

Mary woke early and rushed to get dressed before the others, but Martha and Lazarus were already up and in the midst of their chores. Asa had even left for the fields.

"I thought I would be prompt this morning, but it looks like everyone had the same idea," she said, greeting her siblings with kisses.

"We wanted to surprise you," Martha said. "Lazarus decided that we can go to Galilee right after the Sabbath."

Mary's heart soared for a second and then plopped back to earth with a thud. "That will be two more days. What if Jesus moves on before then?"

Martha and Lazarus stared at Mary as if she had just slapped them.

"That is the soonest we are able to go," Martha explained. "Tonight, we will celebrate Shabbat supper, and tomorrow we rest. We can leave early the morning after that."

Lazarus nodded. "What else would you have us do?"

Mary chewed on her lips for a moment and then reasoned that there was no other option. Even if Lazarus had conceded last night, they wouldn't be able to get to Jesus any sooner.

That decided, Mary perked up and went about her morning chores. Though she no longer fetched the water alone, with a new portico to sweep, Mary had plenty to do. She had most of her work done by lunch time and still managed to get some weaving done before she began her Shabbat preparations.

As she was helping Martha wash the platter for the table, she heard a donkey bray outside. She rushed to the window to see Tirzah and Josiah, along with another girl, guiding their cart to their house.

The sisters hurried out to greet their friend. "Welcome, Tirzah, come in and rest," Martha said.

Tirzah stood and smiled at the house. "I want to look for a moment," she said. She patted Josiah on the shoulder. "You and your men did well."

Josiah bowed and began unloading several packages from the cart.

Mary raised her brows and gasped at the sight of the things in Josiah's arms. "What is all of this?" she asked after hugging her friend.

Tirzah gestured to the cart and shrugged. "I found some things at the market that might fit well in your home."

Lazarus rounded the far end of the house to greet them.

He froze in place when he saw Josiah unloading a rolled-up rug and taking it into his home.

"Tirzah, you must stop this," he said. Lazarus hurried to her side and shook his head. "To owe so much. I cannot begin to repay."

Tirzah only smiled and took his hand. She pressed her forehead against it. "You are mistaken. Nothing I do or have done brings with it a debt of any kind. When I think of what my son stole from your sister, I shudder with grief." She looked up at Lazarus and nodded. "I do not imagine that any gift I offer could ever repay that injury."

Lazarus led her into the house, and Martha and Mary followed closely behind. The girl stayed to help Josiah bring in the rest of the packages.

Tirzah went on. "I am a woman who was blessed with material wealth, if not with a great family. I would like to use my possessions to help others. Would you deprive me of this?"

Martha looked at Lazarus and shrugged. "I tried to tell you she is not easy to dissuade."

Lazarus wiped at his eyes. "But there are others with greater need," he said.

"Yes, and I will help them as I meet them," Tirzah replied. "For now, please allow me this joy."

Mary tilted her head to one side and sighed, then suddenly remembered. "Tonight, the Sabbath begins. Will you stay with us?"

Tirzah nodded. "I hoped I would not be intruding."

Martha smiled broadly. "We welcome you."

Lazarus gestured to Josiah. "Come. We can put the animals away before the sun sets."

Josiah left with Lazarus and Mary nodded to the girl at Tirzah's side. "What is your name?" Mary asked.

Tirzah laughed. "I almost forgot. This is Vera. She is Josiah's younger sister."

Mary smiled at the young girl and studied her dark eyes and serious expression. "Welcome, Vera."

"Thank you, Mistress." Vera's tiny voice reminded Mary of a bird chirping.

Martha glanced at the window and jumped to her feet. "Forgive me, but there is still much to do before sundown. Mary, will you help me?"

Mary nodded and smiled at Tirzah and Vera. "Please be comfortable."

Tirzah shook her head and nudged the girl. "Vera will help you prepare the meal. She is very skilled in the kitchen. And I will unpack a few things, with your permission."

Martha nodded. "You bring us too much. You have made work for yourself."

The house soon filled with the aromas of the savory meal. Lazarus recited the blessing, and later he and Josiah spoke of Jerusalem and matters of the Temple. They all enjoyed their supper and then retired to the portico.

"I come out here every night now," Mary told Tirzah.

"You need a bench," the older woman suggested.

"Yes, Martha and I were just saying the same thing."

Tirzah nodded to Josiah, and Mary noticed. "No, you must not bring us a bench. We will find one on our own," Mary said.

Tirzah laughed. "All right. You may furnish your own house."

They talked about the warm weather for a while, and Lazarus told Josiah about the bargain he had made with Jeb. "If you know of anyone needing work, I will have a few positions right away, and many more at harvest."

Tirzah squeezed Mary's hand. "I am glad to see a house filled with hope. I am doubly pleased that it is your house."

Martha gestured to the door. "We can go back inside to visit if you like."

Tirzah nodded and followed her hostess back to the table. "Thank you for allowing me to give," she said.

Martha smiled and reached out for her sister's hand. "You have become part of our family. You have seen us in the valleys of despair, and now you are with us in the warmth of our joy."

Mary nodded in agreement. "You have helped to restore our hope."

Tirzah noticed the alabaster box on the shelf and gestured to it. Mary went to get it and placed it on the table in front of Tirzah. "What is in the box?" Mary asked.

Tirzah held it up next to the oil lamp, and the stone box seemed to glow. "It contains a full pint of Spikenard oil. It is sealed in the box for a special occasion."

"What occasion?" Mary asked.

Tirzah placed the fragile container back on the table and then moved Mary's hands around it. "This oil is precious. It is used for perfume and for medicine. The aroma is full and soothing. Some use the fragrance for brides; others use it to anoint the honored dead. It may be included in spices for wines or other foods. It helps bring rest to the weary."

Mary stared at the box between her fingers. "Why did you give it to me?"

Tirzah gazed on Mary's face with a sympathetic expression. "To make the oil, the perfumer must take the root of the flower and press it into a pulp, and then distil the mash and the liquid. It is a long process, and to make a full pint takes many plants. The gardener must tend each plant carefully because only the healthiest plants produce oil sweet enough to sell for perfume."

Mary didn't understand why she explained all of this to her. She waited for Tirzah to continue.

"My mother gave this box to me when I married Gad. She told me that every woman should have something to offer a good man."

Tears formed in Mary's eyes, so she shifted her gaze back to the box.

"I kept the box unopened. I will not speak against my husband, only that I kept the box unopened. I had always intended to give it to my daughter-in-law. But as time passed, I knew that it would never be opened, so long as it remained in my house."

Mary noticed Martha dabbing at her eyes, too. Tirzah's words landed softly on their ears and on their hearts.

"When I knew what Omar had done to you, I knew that I must give it to you." Tirzah patted Mary's hand. "You had almost nothing, but what you had, my son took away. I wanted to give you this, not as payment, but because you needed it. I am not sure what I thought at first."

Martha rose from the table and walked to the window. Mary wondered if this was all too much for her to hear. She wanted to hold Martha's hand, but she didn't dare move from her place.

Vera moved noiselessly to Martha's side. "May I bring you a cup of water, Mistress?" she asked.

Martha smiled and shook her head. "No, I am all right."

Tirzah took a deep breath, and Mary thought that she might be finished, but then the older woman added, "This box is worth about a year's wages. It will make a good dowry estate for you if you find a good man. If you choose to marry."

Mary stared in disbelief at the box. Her tears dried quickly. For weeks, this box had resided next to the cooking oil. Mary's heart beat loudly in her ears as she realized its value.

Tirzah must have noticed her expression change. She said, "The value is not in the cost of the perfume, my dear. The value is in finding a good man on which to spend it. I believe in you. I trust that when you meet that man, you will know."

Mary pulled the box to her bosom and allowed the tears to flow. "Thank you, Tirzah. Your faith in my future is the greatest gift I know."

FOURTEEN

Tirzah, Vera, and Josiah left for Jerusalem as Lazarus, Martha, and Mary headed north to the Sea of Galilee. Asa stayed home to manage the fields.

"I wonder what kinds of things he will say." Mary chattered as they began their trip. "Asa said that Jesus talks about many different subjects. Maybe it will be a story."

Martha smiled and nodded, already feeling the heat of the bright sunlight. "I hope we have enough food for the trip. It has been a long time since we last went to the Sea."

Lazarus laughed. "I am confident we will have plenty. You always see to that, sister." He raised his hand to shield his eyes as he studied the sky. "I am more concerned about the weather."

"Do you think it will rain?" Martha asked.

Mary twirled a circle in her path, turning her face to the sun. "The sky is beautiful and clear. No rain in sight."

Lazarus slowed his pace and gestured to the hills far to the north. "Do you see the dark fringe coming over the mountains there?"

Martha squinted and nodded. "Yes, I see that. But is that not just a cloud?"

Lazarus sighed. "Yes, but it is a cloud that may stretch for miles and miles. One cloud, with the right wind behind it, can cause lots of trouble on the waters of Galilee."

Mary scoffed. "But the Sea of Galilee is a few day's journey away."

"A day's journey for man is but an hour for God's hand." Lazarus resumed his normal gait but kept his attention on the sky.

Martha slowed Mary's pace by reaching out and taking her hand. She smiled at Mary and said, "We should think about where we might like to stay when we reach the crowds. We have a tent with us. Should we choose a place near the water, or perhaps under some trees for shade?"

Mary drew a deep breath and exhaled loudly. "I think either will be wonderful. I just want to hear Jesus again." She smiled at her brother and sister. "Do you think he will really come to visit us at our house?"

Martha tilted her head and shrugged. "Do not raise your hopes too high, Mary. Jesus is a busy man. He may have many others to see in Bethany, or he may not come near Bethany again for quite a while."

Lazarus nodded. "Nicodemus is concerned about him. Says he stirs up trouble wherever he goes."

Mary shook her head. She didn't want her brother to speak

like that. She took the bag that she carried and slung the strap over her shoulder so both her hands would be free. She reached out to Lazarus's hand and walked with both her brother and sister, holding hands three across as when they were children.

"I know that we have only seen Jesus once and that he barely spoke to us at all, but he did say that he would come." Mary squeezed both their hands. "I believe him."

"Yes, well I would like to see him and learn more about him before I invite him to my supper table. Nicodemus is a reasonable man. If he has reservations, then I do, too."

Mary rolled her eyes, but she knew that her brother meant well. She also knew that if he actually disapproved of Jesus, then he would never have agreed to go and hear him speak. Her heartbeat kept pace with her footsteps. She found herself wanting to run.

In a few more days they would see him again. *Mary* would see him again. She couldn't seem to stop her lips from smiling.

Martha laughed at her. "Mary, calm yourself. I can practically feel your fingers throbbing in my hand. Jesus will be there when we get there."

"I am going to walk right up to him and thank him for what he has already done for me," Mary said. "And if anyone asks me about him, I will tell them that Jesus healed me. He gave me a miracle."

Martha nodded. "Mary, must I remind you again? He is an important man. You cannot bother him."

"Perhaps you are right," Mary said. "He must have hundreds of others to heal and to bless. I should stay out of his way so that others may enjoy the same miracles as me, but I really should thank him."

For three days, the siblings walked and talked about what they saw, and what they might see when they reached Jesus. The travel was easy, and they had plenty of food, though after the second night sleeping in the tent, they all began to miss their beds.

Mary chattered with excitement as they got closer to Galilee. Martha seemed to listen, but never added anything more than a nod here and there. Lazarus maintained his watch on the sky and the clouds that seemed to grow and darken. Mary decided to ignore them. Lazarus watched the sky enough for all of them.

Martha and Lazarus slowed their steps considerably. Mary looked ahead and saw the multitude of people ahead.

"We must be getting near," Mary said. "We should hurry."

Martha tightened her grip on Mary's hand. Mary frowned. She felt like a child under the strict control of her mother.

"I want to get closer," Mary insisted.

Martha pressed her lips into a thin, tight line. "We should stay together. Crowds invite trouble."

Mary remembered her father warning them with those words whenever they would go to the busy marketplace. She didn't need to be told what was dangerous and what wasn't. "I am not a child, Martha."

Lazarus raised one brow and narrowed his gaze. "You are a grown woman, that is true, but we should still stay together."

"I will stay with both of you, but please may we get closer. We will never be able to hear Jesus over this crowd. And we certainly cannot see him from here."

Lazarus nodded and took the lead. He pulled Mary behind him, and Martha hemmed her in from behind.

All around her, Mary could hear people talking about Jesus. They whispered marvelous things about seeing signs from God, hearing him speak about a great harvest, and how he was going to heal this person or that. Mary wanted to add her story to theirs, but she didn't intend to slow down until she saw him again with her own eyes.

She felt that they were getting closer because the noise from the people grew louder. She wondered if he would remember her. It had been nearly a month since she had been healed. She wanted to tell everyone she saw that she was made clean and whole by him.

Her heart slammed in her chest at the sheer energy she felt from the others. The crowd pressed closer. She knew Jesus was near. She walked on her tip-toes as she followed her brother. She tried to see over the heads of the other people, but it seemed that everyone was standing as tall as they could.

And then, when her calves ached from stretching, and she couldn't walk any farther, she saw him. For a split-second, her heart soared with exhilaration, but the next moment it sank with a thud.

Jesus was getting into a boat, and telling the men with him to row out from shore. She was too late.

FIFTEEN

They had come such a long way, only to see him drift out to sea.

But that wasn't what was happening at all. Mary watched as the crowds of people began to sit in the sand, waiting for Jesus to speak. Mary looked at Martha and Lazarus and nodded.

Martha quickly pulled out the rolled blanket from Lazarus's pack and stretched it out on the ground. The crowds were so great that the beach soon became one endless stretch of mats and blankets, one corner overlapping another, each covered with another family to see Jesus.

Mary watched as the entire shoreline filled with people from all over the countryside. Young, old, healthy, and the sickly waited in growing silence as Jesus found the right place on the water.

Everyone seemed eager to hear. Mary wondered how

many of them had already been touched by Jesus. How many others had already been healed?

She listened carefully when he began. His voice didn't boom or cry out. The water allowed him to speak in a normal tone, carrying his words perfectly to the whole gathering.

Jesus spoke of planting seeds, and Mary watched Lazarus's expression grow serious. There was a story of a man with a field plagued with rocks, hard soil, thorns, and crows. Mary knew that Lazarus understood these hazards. Jesus told about how some seed fell on the good soil of the field, and what a bountiful crop those seeds produced.

Mary realized that the story had a much greater meaning. Her mind considered all the ways that Jesus' words might apply. She was just a little seed, exposed to hard times. But if she planted herself in good soil, something magnificent would happen. She decided that Jesus had healed her for a reason. God had a wonderful plan for her life. She knew it in her heart.

Jesus went on to speak about many more things, each subject reassuring to Mary that she was part of something important. She was not insignificant or worthless. Mary studied her sister's face and then her brother's. She saw a change come over them. She looked around at the strangers sitting next to them. Some had confused expressions. A few looked angry. Many were shrouded in desperation, but most held a sense of calm. Mary knew that they shared the same sense of peace that she felt.

After nearly an hour of speaking, Jesus offered a blessing to the crowd and then instructed the men with him to take the boat to the other side of the sea. Mary knew their time was over.

She hadn't been able to speak with Jesus again, but hearing him talk was enough for now.

Lazarus peered up at the sky as the crowd dispersed. "We should find a place to camp for the night. The clouds are building, and we cannot travel in a storm."

Martha and Lazarus found a place up the hill from the shore. There were plenty of trees for shelter, with a small clearing for the tent. In another hour, their home for the night was up, and Martha was preparing their supper.

"I hope you are not too disappointed that you did not talk to him," Martha said as she handed the basket of bread to Mary.

"Oh no, it was beautiful to hear him again."

Lazarus motioned to the tent. "I hope it will stand through the storm."

Martha and Mary gathered up the food and the cooking utensils just as a massive wind whipped through the trees. The gust was so strong that their meager fire blew out. The three siblings sat within the small canvas structure eating their supper and listening to the storm howl.

Within a few minutes, the rain began. Large, heavy drops pounded the sides of the tent, competing with the wind to make more noise. Lazarus sat facing the door flap, ready to re-secure the closure if the wind blew it open. Mary and Martha huddled together, watching for leaks or tears. The wind pushed and pulled at the canvas. The ropes moaned, and the grounding pegs strained to keep the small residence in place.

Mary could hear Lazarus praying for peace. She joined with him, praying in her heart when suddenly she thought about Jesus. He and his men were out on the lake in this storm. A flash of light and the crack of thunder rolled over the water and up the side of the hill.

Mary prayed earnestly for all the men on the water, and especially for Jesus. How could their small fishing vessel withstand this kind of torrent?

Mary squeezed Martha's hand. "I am worried for Jesus and the others on the boat."

Martha smiled, but it appeared to be forced. "They seemed to be seasoned fishermen. I am sure that they made shore before the weather turned."

Mary tried to believe it, but in her heart, she felt sure that they were still in the middle of the Sea.

The wind grew even stronger, and the back corner of the tent pulled free from the stake. All three jumped up to grab the furiously flapping canvas. Lazarus took hold and threw himself to the ground, trying to prevent the whole thing from flying away. Mary and Martha caught the edge on either side of their brother and pulled the seams to the ground.

To hold her side in place, Mary gripped the seam tightly and then rolled her whole body over the fabric, securing the edge of the tent between herself and the damp ground. The canvas became like porous linen, and the rain soaked through, drenching Mary to the skin. Martha held her edge still enough for Lazarus to drive another stake through the corner.

"If the storm continues like this, we will not be able to

hold the tent together. The seams are straining as it is," Lazarus said.

Martha looked scared. Mary had not seen her this frightened since the fire. She knew that Martha did not like for situations to be out of her control. Mary continued to pray.

"Lord, almighty Yahweh, King of the universe, please hear us." Mary started praying aloud. She stopped at the sudden silence.

Without warning, the storm died, and the night around them was completely quiet. There was no wind pulling the tent canvas from their hands. There was no more rain. No more lightning or thunder. The only sound Mary could hear was Lazarus, Martha, and herself, gasping for breath.

They all released their grips on the tent edges. Mary sat up and looked around, waiting. Lazarus and Martha just stared at each other with their mouths open and their eyes wide.

"What happened?" Mary asked.

Lazarus shook his head and dared to open the flap door. He poked his head outside, and then quickly turned back to face his sisters. "Come and see."

He walked outside and motioned for Mary and Martha to join him. Mary followed her sister outside to see a canopy of brilliant stars shining down from the heavens.

The nearly full moon lit up the night, reflecting off the mirror-still surface of the water. Mary didn't understand.

"What happened to the storm? The clouds?" she asked.

"The wind?" Martha added.

Lazarus shrugged. "Who can say?"

Other people were coming out of tents nearby. Some

were already packing up the ruins of their all-but-destroyed sites.

"Look at the Sea," another man said. He walked to the water's edge. "The surface is like polished silver."

Lazarus and a few others joined him, and Mary could hear them talking.

"What would cause a storm to suddenly stop like that?" one asked.

"I have never known it to happen," another added.

Mary walked around their tattered tent, tugging at her dress to keep it from clinging to her shivering body. She squeezed at the loose folds to wring out the excess rainwater. She looked up to see Martha doing the same.

"At least, the night air is warm," Martha said with a laugh.

"But the rain was cold."

Mary looked out at the water, wishing she could see something. But even with the bright moon and calm waters, nothing could be seen on the lake. The sea appeared to dissolve into black, blending inseparably into the stars.

Martha placed a damp hand against Mary's cheek. "I am sure that Jesus and his boat found a safe harbor."

Mary nodded. "I hope so."

C H A P T E R

SIXTEEN

The trip back to the nearest town seemed long, and Mary was exhausted from the storm. Martha and Lazarus discussed whether to find an inn or to travel on. Lazarus wanted to find a room and rest for another day before beginning the long trip. Martha thought they should go on. She said that with the tent in disrepair, they should watch their money more carefully and keep inn stays at a minimum.

Mary paid attention to their discussion only half-heartedly. Instead, she did her best to listen to other travelers' conversations about the strange squall at sea. She heard no reports of shipwrecks or other damage.

Deciding to journey on to the next town, they stopped at a well to refill their water skins. Lazarus went to find a room for them at an inn on the southernmost edge of the city. Waiting on the street, Mary overheard some men talking.

"They said he was heading back to the Decapolis this evening," one said.

"Everywhere he goes, people follow. He is a great healer, they say," the other one replied.

"I heard some saying that he was going to bring down the Temple."

"Talk like that will land him in prison," a third man added.

Mary strained to hear a name.

"Too many people love him. He keeps a close company of friends around him. And a group of women who pay for his work."

"Women travel with him?"

The first man nodded. "Yes. I hear it over and over. When Jesus of Nazareth says, 'Follow me,' people do."

Mary felt a surge of energy. She wanted to ask them more, but she knew that kind of behavior was unacceptable and dangerous, especially with strangers. For now, she would be happy knowing that he had survived the storm.

"Sisters, come," Lazarus said, motioning for Mary and Martha to follow him. "We have a room just down here."

Once inside, Mary announced. "I heard a man say that Jesus was on his way to the Decapolis. He is safe. He may even be there now."

Lazarus sighed. Mary knew that he was at least as tired as she was. "Mary, I hope you are right that he is safe. But have we sunk to listening to others gossip? And how can you be sure of whom they spoke? There are lots of men named Jesus."

"The man said, 'Jesus of Nazareth' and he called him a

great healer. I know he was speaking of *our* Jesus." Mary's face beamed with joy that couldn't be deflated with any of her brother's practicality.

"He is *our* Jesus now?" Martha said with a raised brow.

"You know what I mean," Mary insisted. "And just hearing that good news lightens my heart."

Martha loosened her head scarf and pushed her fingers through her thick black hair. "I think we will all sleep better knowing he is well."

Lazarus nodded. "I am glad to hear it. But now we must sleep. We still have two days of travel, and we are already tired."

Mary kissed Martha and Lazarus good night and stretched out on her blanket. She pressed her eyes closed and tried not to think about anything. She wanted to get right to sleep. But sleep was elusive.

Mary's thoughts wandered from Jesus' stories from the boat to the crowds of people aching for healing. She thought about how his voice calmed her, both the first time she heard it and the last. She remembered how the madness in her brain was like the thunderous storm they endured the night before. The howling wind that filled her thoughts with confusion and doubt. The rain of shame that battered every hope of a future. The thunder of guilt and helplessness that finally fractured her soul. They were all voices in her ears, screams and whispers. And then she heard his quiet voice that stilled her storm.

"You are clean," he said. Mary could almost hear it again. And it was true.

She stared at the ceiling, though in the darkness she

couldn't see anything. She could hear Martha breathing steadily. She could hear Lazarus, too, though he sounded more like a sleeping lion, with a deep rumbling purr.

Mary thought about her childhood, and she missed her parents. She tried to imagine what they might say about Jesus of Nazareth. They were always very practical like Lazarus was now. But Mary knew that they would be interested in hearing Jesus speak. Her mother always liked a good story.

She would hold Martha and Mary in her lap and tell them about Joseph being sold as a slave and carried off to Egypt. She would recount about Moses leading God's people to the land of milk and honey. She would sing the song of Deborah and the song of Miriam and the many psalms of David.

Mary imagined her mother singing her favorite song to her now.

"Oh Yahweh, our Lord, how majestic is your name in all the earth. You have set your glory in the heavens," she would sing.

Mary closed her eyes as the words of her mother hung heavy in her ears and light in her heart.

CHAPTER

SEVENTEEN

Four more days of walking brought more news about Jesus. It seemed that everywhere they went Mary overheard people talking about him healing the blind, deaf, or lame, or even feeding multitudes with a small basket of food.

"A man such as this could solve the whole region's problems," she heard in the market of one village.

"Imagine no sickness and no hunger," in another town.

"A man like this could challenge Caesar."

"A man like Jesus should be Caesar," she heard over and over.

She pondered the idea of the man who had healed her sitting on a throne. He didn't seem like one to issue proclamations or negotiate treaties. He was more like a man who just cared for others more than he cared for himself.

After hours of thinking such things over, she decided that she didn't like hearing people talk about Jesus in such ways.

Though many comments were praising, there were others that suggested that Jesus was overstepping his position.

"He speaks with authority, but he holds no official position. That kind of arrogance will bring him trouble," Mary heard a man say as they passed by on the road.

Mary tried to linger to hear more, but Lazarus and Martha kept too quick of pace. The conversation of trouble brought worry to Mary's mind. *Jesus is kind and wise. He offers only hope and healing. Why must people be cruel? Why must they assume the worst of others?*

She walked on, deep in thought, until she realized how close they were to Jerusalem. She could see the giant wall of the city just ahead, reaching up to the sky. They would be back in Bethany before sunset.

Martha took her hand as they reached the gates. Their path home led past Gad's caravansary. "Keep your eyes down as we pass," she told Mary.

Mary nodded and moved to the opposite side of the road. She needn't have worried about being recognized or even noticed. The merchants were busy with loads of goods, with crates and camels, and with barking orders to every kind of servant. Mary and Martha followed Lazarus through the market and down the hill toward the gate that faced home.

"Do you want a large supper tonight?" Martha asked Lazarus.

"I am hungry, but I believe I am even more tired. You are exhausted, too. We should just have a small supper and go quickly to bed," Lazarus said with a slight moan.

Mary knew he was tired. In the last two days, he had developed a rasp in his voice from the dusty road.

"Just a bit of stew then?" Martha asked.

Lazarus shook his head. "It is too warm for stew, sister. Perhaps some dried fish and some vegetables from the garden."

Mary nodded. "I expect you will have many cucumbers ready to pick by now." She smiled at her sister. Martha knew how much Mary loved a juicy sweet cucumber on a warm summer evening.

Martha squeezed her hand. "It will be nice to be home."

"To sleep in our own beds," Mary added.

"Amen," Lazarus said. "We should walk a little faster. There is still plenty of sunlight, but the evening hours are approaching. The Jericho Road can be dangerous."

Mary noticed how quickly the road traffic lightened once they left the east gate and headed down the hills. "Bethany is no one's destination but ours," she said.

Lazarus laughed until he brought up a short cough. "Most people would prefer to avoid a town dedicated to the poor and sickly."

Martha knit her brows and placed her hand on Lazarus's shoulder. "With that cough, it seems appropriate for you to go there."

"I am not ill, Martha. Just a little dirt in my throat. A good night's sleep will cure me." He pointed to their house. "The sight of our home does more good than a doctor's remedy."

Mary looked up to see their larger-than-she-remembered house. Asa stood at the door with a water jar in his hands. As they came closer, he put it down and waved.

"We are back, my friend!" Lazarus called.

Asa turned and leaned in the door and then hurried back out to greet them on the path. He took their packs and their bags from them and led them to the portico. Mary saw a bench against the wall of the house.

"Martha, look! We have a bench."

Martha shook her head. "I told Tirzah not to send one."

Lazarus interrupted. "This is not from Tirzah. I asked Asa to build it while we were gone. It is a surprise for my favorite sisters."

"Thank you, Lazarus," Mary and Martha said together.

"Please sit," Asa said. "We will wash your feet out here."

Martha smiled and gestured to her brother. "Lazarus first."

Asa bowed to Martha and smiled. "Please, if all three will sit."

Martha and Mary joined Lazarus on the bench, and Asa went inside for a minute. When he returned, he was followed by Vera, who carried a basin and a towel.

Mary smiled. "Vera, it is wonderful to see you again, but what are you doing here?"

Vera nodded to Asa, who explained. "Josiah brought her a few days ago. Tirzah decided that she needed to work in your household."

"This is too much, " Martha began.

Asa continued. "Tirzah wants her here for many reasons. First, as you see, Vera is a beautiful young girl. Tirzah and Josiah both fear for her safety if she stays in the house with Omar. Second, if she is living here, Tirzah and Josiah have a good reason to visit regularly. They will need to check on her from time to time. You will be granting them all a favor."

Vera nodded. "Most of all, you will be showing favor to me."

Mary and Martha smiled, and Mary reached out to take Vera's hand. "Then you are most welcome to our family."

Asa and Vera washed the siblings' feet, and then they all went inside. A feast of fresh vegetables, bread, and cheese waited for them on the table. Martha almost cried when she realized there was nothing for her to prepare.

"I suppose that I am more tired than I thought," she said.

"You must tell us of your journey," Asa said. "Your tent roll was ripped. You must have a great story about that."

Lazarus began by telling about the long walk to the sea. He went on about seeing Jesus and how disappointed they were that they had missed speaking with him. Then he began telling about the storm.

"How frightened you must have all been," Asa said.

Vera's wide eyes told the others that she was concerned as well.

"The women were, of course," Lazarus said.

Martha laughed. "We have been in storms before. The strange part was how the storm ended."

Mary nodded and leaned forward. "The squall raged for nearly an hour, and then was dead silent the next minute."

"What do you mean?" Asa asked.

Lazarus nodded. "Just as she said. Calm and quiet as a Sabbath morning. Not a cloud in the sky or a ripple on the lake."

"How can that be?" Vera's shoulders hunched forward as she listened.

"Nobody knows," Lazarus answered. "No one could

explain it."

A shudder ran down Mary's spine just thinking about it again.

"And that is how the tent was torn?" Asa asked.

"Yes," Martha said with a nod. "I will see about mending it this week." She looked around her tidy house. "It is good to be back in a solid house."

Lazarus nodded in agreement. "Yes. And we are glad to say that the journey home was uneventful."

Mary rolled her eyes. "Lazarus, you forgot to mention that we heard people talking as we returned. They said that Jesus and his men were safe from the storm, too. Perhaps we will see him again soon."

Lazarus sighed. "After hearing some of the talk, I hope Jesus will stay clear of Jerusalem for a while. Some say he stirs up too much trouble. People want him to challenge Caesar or, at least, Herod. The soldiers are just waiting for zealots or one of the other sects to give them an excuse to come down on the Jews."

Asa chewed on his lower lip. "Yes, he would do well to keep to Galilee for a bit."

Mary frowned. "Well, I hope he comes back to this region. Jesus does not have to stay in Jerusalem. He could speak at the Jordan River again. He could remain in Bethany. Nobody in Jerusalem cares one iota what happens in Bethany."

"That is nearly true," Lazarus said.

Mary was about to say more when she noticed Martha trying to suppress a yawn. She couldn't help but join her, and soon everyone had released a wide yawn.

"Martha, could you manage a blessing over the family?" Lazarus asked.

Martha smiled and offered the evening blessing. Her brother joined her in a prayer of thanksgiving for their safe journey, and for the presence of Asa and Vera. A collective "amen" rose from them all, followed closely by another yawn.

"I think it is time for bed," Martha announced.

Mary gathered up the dishes. "I will clean up."

Martha and Vera offered to help, but Mary insisted. "You should both go ahead. I may be tired, but my head is so full of thoughts and wonders that it may be another hour before I can sleep."

The men laughed and headed upstairs. Vera helped Martha get ready for bed, and Mary washed the cups and platters and straightened the table.

A single thought kept repeating in her mind. "Jesus, come back soon." Over and over it tumbled, at times sounding urgent and at others falling more like a song in her ears. Though she couldn't seem to quiet the phrase, she didn't fear it as she had the other voices from before. This was not the sound of torment. This was a simple meditation of her heart.

When she finished her chores, she went into the bedroom. Martha and Vera were already fast asleep in their beds. She dressed for bed and combed her hair. Mary stretched out on her blankets and stared at the stars through her window. She was glad to be home, but she wanted much more.

Jesus, come back soon.

CHAPTER

EIGHTEEN

Another week passed, and Mary could speak of little else except making their home ready for Jesus to visit. She spent hours working at her loom, making blankets and table covers. She decided to make a few extra to send with Jesus and his followers on their travels.

Martha worked to get their house in order, and they found Vera to be a tremendous help. Lazarus and Asa labored in the fields almost every day, and the crops were starting well. For the first time in two years, Mary saw real hope in her brother's attitude.

"Do you think that Jesus will come near Bethany again," Vera asked Mary.

"I think he will. Many people need him," Mary said. She folded another stack of blankets and put them on the chest near the bedroom door. "I hope he will, anyway."

Vera shrugged. "I wish that I could have seen him. If he does come, I would like to go."

"I will make sure that you see him." Mary patted her shoulder. "Once you meet him, you will be changed."

"Josiah told me what happened to you," the young girl said. "He said that it was beautiful."

There was a loud rap at the door, and both women jumped to their feet. Before Mary could answer, Martha burst in with Josiah close behind.

"Sister, he is here."

Mary and Vera exchanged glances. "Who?" Mary asked.

Josiah laughed. "Jesus is on his way here now."

"To Bethany?" Vera raised her brows as she ran to her brother's side.

Martha shook her head and pulled Mary to the door. "He is on his way to our house. His friend, John, ran ahead to tell us. They will have supper with us."

Mary could hardly believe her ears. "Jesus is coming."

"There is much to do. They will be here any minute," Martha said.

Josiah nodded. "I will bring Lazarus home from the field."

Martha turned to Vera. "Help in the kitchen. Mary and I will greet them at the door. When the men return, they can host our visitors until we all finish preparing the food."

Mary nodded. She smoothed the front of her robe with her hands and ran out to the portico to wait. Everyone else had something to do, and she waited.

She paced from one end of the portico to the other. She sat on the bench for a second and then hopped back to her feet. She scanned the horizon for her friend. She saw a shadow at the end of the path. The shadow grew. It came closer until she could make out individuals. She saw five or six men. They were talking and laughing.

Mary saw Jesus in the center of the group. She recognized the others as some of the men who were in the boat with him. She couldn't stop smiling as they approached. Martha joined her to greet their visitors.

Mary intended to stay in her place under the porch cover until they reached the house, but she let propriety slip and ran out to greet them. When Jesus saw her, he opened his arms wide.

"Mary, how happy I am to see you again." He took her hands in his and kissed her cheek.

"Shalom," she said, trying not to embarrass Martha. "Welcome to my home. Welcome, all of you." She nodded to the other men.

The youngest of the men led the others to the door. "Thank you, Mary." He nodded to Martha. "And dear Martha, peace be on your house." He bowed his head to her. "My name is John."

"Welcome, John."

Jesus introduced the other men, and Martha asked them to sit on the bench while Mary washed their feet. First Jesus, then John, Peter, Andrew and lastly James allowed her to wash and dry their feet. She invited them inside to meet the others

"Thank you for welcoming us into your house," Jesus told Martha. "Your hospitality is appreciated."

"We are glad to receive you. You have shown such favor

to our sister, we can never repay." Martha gestured to the door as Lazarus and Asa returned with Josiah. "Our brother welcomes you, too."

Lazarus greeted him and exchanged introductions. The men all went to the table to recline. Vera and Josiah went to the well to draw more water.

Mary looked toward the kitchen. Martha efficiently stirred the stew while the bread baked. The vegetables were all chopped and seasoned. The wine was poured. Mary nodded. She knew what she should do.

She picked up the cups and served them to her guests and then to Lazarus and Asa. When she had all the cups placed on the table, she found a seat near Jesus and listened to his story.

"When something is lost," he said, "and it has great value, the owner will pour his whole effort into searching until it is found. That is what a good shepherd does when he has lost a single lamb. That is what we are doing."

Mary nodded. She knew what it was like to be lost. Her heart was full, just thinking that she was valuable to Jesus.

As if he heard her thoughts, Jesus turned to face her. "And when what was lost is found, the celebration is great in Heaven." He smiled. "What a celebration we had when we saw your sister whole again."

He looked at Lazarus, who beamed at Mary. "Yes, you healed not only our Mary but our home as well."

John nodded to Mary and smiled. "Jesus told us that you were a bright light in his day."

Mary blushed.

Peter laughed. "Never be ashamed at being healed from

your brokenness. Everyone has something that needs to be healed. Jesus has come to make everything whole. You have a beautiful story to tell."

Andrew added, "Peter has a story, too."

Mary turned to listen to Peter. "Yes," he began. "My wife's mother was ill last week. She had a fever and could not even stand without fainting. Jesus took her hand and healed her." He patted Jesus' shoulder. "She got to her feet and proceeded to prepare an excellent supper for us."

Martha took the opportunity to say, "Jesus, do you see that Mary has left me to prepare supper all by myself? I wish that you would tell her to help me."

Jesus smiled and reached out for Martha's hand. When he touched her, Mary could see Martha's expression change. She saw the worry lines in her sister's forehead fade and smooth.

"Martha, you are concerned about too many things," Jesus said. "You are doing a beautiful thing serving us. Mary knows that it is important to listen; what she is doing is beautiful, too. She has much to learn. Mary has a different path ahead of her. She needs to be hearing me. It will not be taken from her."

Martha nodded to Mary and smiled to Jesus.

She went back to ladling the stew into bowls. Mary could see that now Martha listened more carefully to what the men were saying.

"Were you in the storm, on the lake, I mean, during the storm?" Mary asked. "We were concerned."

James coughed through a laugh. "Yes, and we were concerned, too."

James and John told them about the storm, and how Jesus had fallen asleep, exhausted after speaking to the crowds. They told how he woke and told the storm to stop, and it did.

Mary stared in awe. Martha blinked to stifle tears. Lazarus began to laugh. "What did you do?" Lazarus asked Jesus' friends.

Peter shook his head. "We prayed. We worshiped. We may have cried. Some of us may have."

Josiah and Vera returned and helped Martha bring the food to the table. Everyone sat while Lazarus offered the blessing.

Jesus talked about where they had been and what they had done. Lazarus asked about where they planned to go next.

James and Andrew shared a worried expression. John seemed to ignore their concerns. "We go where God leads us."

"My Father has a plan," Jesus said.

"Are you a prophet?" Mary asked. She had waited for someone to explain more, but she was getting impatient.

"What do you believe?" Jesus asked her.

Mary looked at this man who had healed her. She wanted to blurt out an answer, but she felt her brother's and sister's critical gazes on her. Could she speak what her heart felt?

Peter tapped the table in front of Mary. "Do not be afraid. You know."

"You cannot be only a prophet." Mary swallowed hard.

"Could a prophet calm a storm on a lake? No. And who calms a storm in a girl's mind?"

Martha took a deep breath. "Messiah?" she whispered.

Lazarus began to cough. Mary guessed that her brother must be worried about what his friends at the Temple would say.

Jesus looked at Mary and then at Martha. "Thank you for welcoming us into your home." He nodded toward Lazarus. "Your sisters have a great gift for serving. They see more, and they understand more than many others."

Mary leaned closer toward Jesus. "You have women who travel with you, too?"

"Some do," Jesus answered. He looked at Mary. "They see opportunities that might otherwise go unnoticed. They are like you."

Mary nodded. She understood what he meant. Women often see needs that men miss. She longed to ask if she could go, too.

Jesus smiled and faced Lazarus. "Mary would be very helpful in my work."

Mary turned to her brother with a pleading look in her eyes. When she woke up that morning, she never imagined asking her brother if she could leave her home for a time. Now all she wanted was to travel with Jesus and learn. She wanted to help serve the people he would heal. She wanted to know more about the Messiah's plan.

"Please, Lazarus," Mary said.

Jesus faced Mary and stared straight into her dark, pleading eyes. "There is work for you here in Bethany that would advance my message a hundred-fold. There is work for you all here."

Lazarus appeared more than concerned. "Will you all stay here tonight?" he asked. "We have a large room upstairs. This will give us time to talk."

Peter almost laughed. "I remember when Jesus asked us to follow him."

Jesus stopped him. "Everyone has a different path of service."

Peter nodded in respect. "You are right."

"We will stay the night. You are gracious," Jesus said.

Lazarus led the men upstairs to their room. Mary, Martha, and Vera cleaned downstairs.

"Will Lazarus allow me to serve?" Mary asked Martha. "Will you?"

Martha didn't answer. Mary shot a glance toward Vera, who avoided eye contact with both of them.

"I did not mean to cause you embarrassment, sister," Mary insisted. "I just could not tear myself away from his side. You heard all the things he said. You saw how he was, and who he is."

Martha nodded. "I saw it. I saw you. I was a little hurt at first, but not too hurt to know that Jesus was right. The look on your face was like when you were a child. It was like seeing you again at our father's knee, listening to his stories."

Mary took her sister's hand. "Will you talk to Lazarus? All I want to do is be a follower, a disciple of Jesus."

Lazarus came downstairs to speak to them. He frowned

as he took his place at the table. Vera nodded to them and excused herself to the bedroom.

"Brother, please do not make your decision before considering the possibilities," Mary started.

Lazarus coughed again. "Mary, I will be fair. I will listen. But you must abide by my decision. Do you understand?"

"Yes, I understand," she replied. She said a quick prayer in her heart. *Yahweh God, please help Lazarus to understand.*

CHAPTER

NINETEEN

Mary woke before sunrise, anxious to see what the day held. To her surprise, most of the household were already awake and bustling with activity.

She saw Lazarus sitting out on the portico, and when he saw her, he motioned for her to join him.

"I might as well know now," she whispered to herself.

"Sister," he said as she sat next to him. "I have wrestled with this all night. I know how much Jesus has helped you."

Mary started to interrupt him. She wanted to tell him that he could never imagine how much Jesus actually healed her. She wanted to say how utterly hopeless she had been. How alone and desperate and tortured, but something held her tongue, and so she listened.

"I have also considered what might happen to our family if you become one of his followers, whether you leave home to travel with his company or stay here to do his work in

Bethany." Lazarus appeared nervous as if someone might be spying on this conversation.

Mary took his hand and fixed her gaze on him. He laughed.

"There. This is what you do to others. With just that expression, you make everyone you know feel important. That is one of the gifts that Jesus sees in you."

Mary blushed. "What have you decided? I will abide by your word." She wanted to protest. She wanted to say that whatever his decision, she would follow Jesus anyway.

"You ask me if you can do Jesus' work?" Lazarus smiled and tugged at a curl that had strayed from Mary's head scarf.

"I do, brother."

"I have spent the early hours of this day weighing the cost to our family. What would others think? What would Nicodemus say? When it seems we are just recovering from the valley of shadows, would this pull us down even further?"

Mary watched the lines on Lazarus's forehead deepen with each word. She blinked back the urge to cry. She only waited.

Lazarus took both her hands in hers. "And then I look into your eyes, and I cannot imagine what my life would be like without Jesus. I know that he saved you. I know that without him, I would no longer have you. He brought you back to us. How could I deny you the chance to serve him? How could I deny my opportunity to serve him?"

Mary felt the same awe as she had the night the storm had stopped. Her heart leaped in her chest, and she threw her arms over Lazarus's shoulders and hugged him with all her might. "Thank you, brother. Thank you."

He hugged her for several seconds and then shook his head. "It will not be an easy life. Jesus has already faced opposition from almost every angle."

"I know it will be difficult."

Jesus, John, and Peter appeared from around the end of the house. Mary jumped to her feet and ran to them. "Lazarus has agreed."

Jesus smiled at Mary's brother and then back at Mary.

"As if my words made any difference," Lazarus said with a hoarse laugh.

"I told you that I would abide by your decision," Mary insisted.

Lazarus shook his head. "Mary, you may not see it, but the rest of us certainly do. You have already devoted yourself to Jesus and to his message. I doubt anyone has the power to dissuade you now."

Jesus nodded. "You are a mighty little force, Mary. Much stronger than you realize. Your brother and sister see it. We all see it."

"And so what work do you have for me in Bethany?" she asked.

Lazarus led them all into the house to the table where Martha and Vera were already serving breakfast. As they sat, Jesus gestured to the stack of blankets near the door. "You made these?"

Mary nodded. "Yes. Martha and I made them on our mother's old loom. We have set them aside for you and your men to take with you."

John bowed his head toward Mary and then Martha. "You are kind."

Jesus looked back to the table. "And you have served us a breakfast for kings, Martha."

Martha blushed and looked at the floor. "It is humble, but I am happy to do it for you."

Peter exchanged a glance with his brother, Andrew. "Pure hearts," he said.

Jesus turned his focus to Lazarus. "And you, my friend. You protect these women. You provide for them. You would give your last breath for them."

Lazarus stifled a cough. "I have not always been able to give them what they deserve, but I have tried my best. I love my sisters very much."

Jesus nodded. "Bethany is a little town. Poor, and filled with the people too sick to set eyes on the Temple of God. Some are stricken with a disease of the body, and some with a disease of the heart." He looked at Mary.

"I know how the others are aching," she said.

"And who better to offer them hope?" Jesus asked. "To show them what hope looks like?"

Mary watched Lazarus's expression change. He nodded slowly. "We heard you tell a story about a man sowing seed, and how the some fell on rocks, some fell in weeds, and some was plucked up by the birds. And lastly, some fell in fertile soil and grew. I have fields, and I know of what you speak. Only you were not only talking about grain. You were sharing your message."

Jesus and his men smiled. "You are a wise man, Lazarus," Jesus said.

"I do not want to be hard soil, Master." Lazarus looked up to the ceiling. "God help me, I do not want to be hard soil."

"And what will you do now?" John asked.

"I was going to travel to Jerusalem to look for men to work in my field. I was proud," Lazarus confessed. "I wanted to be seen by the prominent leaders in the city as being a benefactor. I wanted to feel important."

Peter raised his brow and nodded.

Lazarus continued. "I was wrong. I will find the men I need in Bethany. Men who are desperate like me. Those are the workers I need. And as they labor beside me, I will tell them about you. They need to know you are here. They need to know there is hope."

Tears poured over Mary's cheeks as she listened to her brother. She looked up to see that Martha was crying, too.

"We have been given much," Martha said. She reached out for Vera's hand. "Josiah's mistress has poured out her heart upon this home. I would like to share our blessings with others." She placed her burned hand on the table, exposing her arm almost to her elbow. "I have hidden myself away. I said it was because I did not want to frighten others, but that it not true. I am the one who is afraid. Afraid of what others will say when they see me."

Lazarus sniffed. Mary could see that now he fought back emotion.

Martha swallowed hard. "But there are plenty of people in Bethany with much greater challenges than mine. Perhaps if I let them see that I am not beaten by my scars, that you have given us a purpose," she said, leaning toward Jesus, "then they will have this same courage. The courage you have shown me."

James and John wore a shared look of awe on their faces. Jesus looked into Martha's eyes, and Mary knew just what she might be experiencing.

"Will you all go into Bethany today, then? May we go with you? Martha and I can take blankets and food to people, and Lazarus can hire some workers." Mary's heart thumped loudly in her ears. She felt a thrill at the idea of walking alongside Jesus and his men.

"We will go," Jesus said, "and you will see what life with us is like."

They all finished breakfast, and Jesus prayed for the group before they left the house for the market in Bethany.

As they passed each little home along the way, Mary thought of the people inside. She said a silent prayer of blessing over the whole village as she walked.

Jesus and his men led the way, with Lazarus at their side. Mary, Martha, and Vera followed closely behind, hemmed in by Josiah and Asa. They stopped at the corner of the market square, and Mary and Martha took their packages of blankets, bread, and food from their garden to the building that served as the hospice for which Bethany was known. A nurse greeted them at the door and thanked them for their donations, and then abruptly turned away and closed the doors.

Mary blinked in shock, and John nodded. "Some will take the gift without seeing the blessing. It is common, but do not worry or become bitter. The seed is planted. That is your job. You cannot always determine the soil upon which it falls."

Mary and Martha looked to Jesus for direction.

"Come, there is still much to do," he assured them.

Lazarus motioned toward a group of men standing in a group. "Here is where I will find my workers."

Jesus and Lazarus approached the men, and Mary could hear her brother negotiating wages with them. She looked around when she heard several shoppers murmuring about Jesus and his company. Within a few minutes, the square buzzed with people coming out to see the healer.

Women brought out their children to be blessed by Jesus, and soon Andrew and Peter were managing a line of sick and desperate people. James and John talked to others in the gathering crowd, telling them about Jesus, and asking them to come to hear him speak in the small garden area away from the market.

Mary realized that everywhere Jesus went, crowds formed. She saw Lazarus and Asa speaking with six men, who soon followed Asa back to the fields to work. Lazarus rejoined the group and began helping Peter with the growing line.

Mary and Martha found themselves helping women hold babies and consoling mothers of sick children. They made their way closer to Jesus as the line progressed. Jesus prayed over children, whose crying stopped. He prayed for exhausted mothers, who left him with fresh joy and energy. He touched the elderly and whispered encouragement into their weary ears.

Mary watched as the line shortened. The people didn't all leave but seemed to wait. She saw one person after another touched and healed and strengthened by Jesus.

"Unclean!" a shout came from the back of the crowd. "Unclean!"

Mary knew exactly what that meant. A leper was coming. Her mind raced as she remembered the fear that had been ingrained in her from childhood. Leprosy killed slowly, ravaging the body as it consumed it.

"Unclean!"

The crowd parted, leaving a wide path to Jesus. Mary saw a man wrapped in bandages and shrouded in tattered clothes slowly approaching. He continued to cry out his warning, as the law required, and Mary could tell by his slurred voice that he had already lost part of his lips to the dreaded disease. As the man walked past her, Mary could smell the foul odor of decay. Her heart broke for the man, and she feared for Jesus.

But Jesus showed no fear. Instead, he reached out as the man got closer.

"Lord, your servant begs your mercy," the leper said. He fell to his knees before Jesus. "I have heard of your power over sickness. If you are willing, I know that you can heal."

Jesus knelt beside the man, placing his hands on the man's shoulders. A gasp of terror went up from the gathering. Mary didn't know whether she gasped or not. She only knew that Jesus should not touch him. Her heart tore in two. She listened as silence filled the square.

She saw Jesus lean close to the man's disfigured face. He pulled the bandages back and touched the open wounds.

"No," she whispered to herself. She saw Jesus share the man's breath as they spoke. She heard Jesus pray, but couldn't make out the words. Just as when he healed her,

Jesus was quiet and intimate. He was speaking only to this man and to God.

She realized that she was clutching her hands together and holding her breath. She saw Jesus pull back the other cloth wraps from the man's hands and arms. The man reached out and held Jesus' hands, bowing low and sobbing.

"Stand up, Simon," Jesus said finally.

The man rose to his feet and Mary could see that he stood several inches taller than he had before he bowed. She saw his face and his hands. They were whole and unblemished. There were no sores or scars. He was healed.

Mary's heart leaped with joy. The man Jesus called Simon stared at his own body. His fingers, all ten of them now, flew to his face. He touched his lips and his nose and realized that they were whole again and healthy. He drew a deep breath and pounded his fists on his chest. He spun around, and the crowd saw him. Another gasp escaped the people, but this time, there was no fear or disgust.

Mary released a sigh of relief and ran to Jesus' side. Martha followed closely behind her. "My Lord," she said to Jesus, and she dropped to her knees.

Jesus took Simon's arm and looked him straight in the eye again. "These women will feed you and make sure you have the clothing you need. You must wash and then show yourself to the priest. You will return to their home and stay until the following Sabbath. Their brother Lazarus will have work for you after that if you need it."

Simon stared at Jesus and nodded. He turned to face Mary and Martha and bowed to them with tears in his eyes. "I am your servant," he said.

Jesus nodded to the women. "John and Josiah will accompany all of you back home. I will see to these people, and will return with my men before supper."

Mary started to object. She wanted to hear Jesus speak to the crowds again. She wanted to stay. After all, Jesus had said that she needed to learn. She needed to hear.

"Yes, Lord," Martha said without hesitation. "We will take care of him."

Martha took Mary's arm, and they led Josiah, John, and Simon back home.

Mary listened as John spoke to Simon about Jesus and his message of hope and forgiveness.

"I have heard many call him trouble," Simon said. "Others call him a teacher or a sorcerer."

"You have seen him now for yourself," John said.

"Yes," Simon said. "And this was not sorcery. This was real. He talked to me. He touched me. When nobody else would. I have not felt another person's touch in years. He was not afraid."

Mary nodded. "Jesus healed me, too. It is a miracle from God."

Simon took her hand. "Yes, it is. A sign and a miracle."

When they reached the house, Josiah and John took Simon upstairs, and Mary and Martha prepared supper. They spoke of nothing else but what they heard and saw that morning. After an hour, the three men joined them, and they all worked together for the evening meal.

Mary noticed that Martha kept looking at Simon with wide eyes. She assumed that it was because of how different he looked after being healed. But then Mary saw that Simon kept glancing at Martha, too. It was not as some stared at her. He didn't study her scars or frown at the idea of her burns. Instead, he seemed to look upon her with admiration and respect. Mary smiled at the thought of someone else seeing her sister as she did.

The door burst open, and Lazarus and Jesus came through, followed closely by James, Peter, and Andrew. Lazarus directed them all to sit, and he stood at the door and watched.

"What has happened?" Martha asked.

"A mob formed," Lazarus said, clearly out of breath. "Some men from Jerusalem came. They listened to Jesus for a while and then stirred up a few more people in the crowd. They began jeering and challenging Jesus."

"Oh, no," Martha said. Her hand flew to her lips, and her brow lowered.

Mary shook her head. "How could they not see what Jesus has done? He was healing them. They were begging for his blessing."

Simon held up his hands. "Did they not see what you did for me?"

Jesus grimaced. Mary could see a mix of pain and sympathy on his face. "Many will see and still not understand. That is how it will always be."

Lazarus coughed for several seconds and then turned away from the window. "I believe we are safe enough now. I was concerned that some may have followed us here." He took a sip of water that Martha handed him to alleviate his cough. "This is what you face every day?"

Peter and the others nodded. Jesus motioned for Lazarus

to sit at his side. "Just because some reject us, does not mean we should stop sharing. Instead, we must realize that the ones who bring the most resistance are the ones for whom our message is most needed."

Lazarus laughed. "You are brave. All of you are brave."

John shook his head. "Who should we fear more? Who should we obey? Men who oppose us or God Almighty who gave us the message?"

Jesus smiled at John and then looked at Simon, Mary, and her family. "You will face struggles ahead in Bethany. Struggles that you cannot imagine right now, but you have a message to share, too."

Martha suddenly looked distressed. "You are leaving us?"

Jesus tilted his head. "We will stay the night, my dear sister. But we must leave tomorrow morning. We will walk with Simon into Jerusalem and then head north. And you, Mary, will stay here and with your sister, you will tend to the people of Bethany."

Mary bit her lip, trying not to cry at the news. "But you will come back?"

Jesus nodded. "Yes, my friends. My dear Mary, you will see us again."

CHAPTER

TWENTY

"Martha, I just feel that keeping it would be selfish." Mary held the box of spikenard oil in her hands like a treasure.

"What do you think should be done with it?" her sister asked. "After all, Tirzah gave it to you for a reason."

Mary sighed. "I know, but Jesus and his men could use it. It is worth a year's wages. Think of what they could do with it." Mary stared at the carved stone box. "People could be helped."

Martha touched her sister's face. "Mary, you care for others much more than for yourself. This gift, this oil, is not just for you. It is for your future. It is for the future of our family." She patted Mary's hand as it covered the top of the box. "Jesus' message is powerful. Yes, you could sell the oil and help a few people for a little while. His message is not dependent on money. It will spread and grow, with or without your money. But Mary, this oil can give you a chance for a husband and children."

Mary nodded and returned the box to the shelf. "I suppose you are right about the message. I only wish that I could do more."

Martha shook her head. "You are helping. We are helping. We are doing what Jesus asks us to do. We are planting seeds."

Lazarus walked through the door and dropped to a cushion at the table. "I need something to drink."

Martha rushed to his side while Mary poured a cup of water for her brother. "What is it?" Martha asked.

Lazarus coughed and pulled at his tunic as if it was choking him. "I cannot seem to catch my breath." He took the cup from Mary and gulped the water down too quickly. He coughed again. "I need to rest for a moment."

Martha put her hand against Lazarus's forehead. "You have a fever. You should go to bed."

Lazarus shook his head. "I have too much to do. It has been seven days. Simon will be back from Jerusalem tonight. Asa needs my help."

Mary refilled the cup with water. "Asa can manage the fields. Martha can handle our guest. I can take care of the house. We just need you to be well."

Lazarus started to stand up. Mary could see the pain on his face as he continued to struggle to breathe without coughing.

"Please, brother."

Martha nodded in agreement.

Lazarus cleared his throat. "I will rest for the day. By

tomorrow, I should be well. This is my job, providing for you."

"And how can you provide for us if you are ill?" Martha asked.

Mary leaned on her brother's shoulder. She could feel the warmth rising from his skin. "You take care of us every day. Please let us take care of you for once."

He smiled and conceded. "I will obey my sisters."

Mary helped him to his feet and led him upstairs to his bed. "We will get you well soon. Jesus has work for us all."

Lazarus nodded and soon drifted to sleep.

Mary listened to his raspy breathing and prayed. "Lord, Yahweh Rapha, You are mighty to heal. Your hand blesses in the morning and the night. Your love endures forever. I pray that you will cover Lazarus with your hand and give him strength."

She spent another hour watching over her brother and praying until she heard voices in the garden. She hurried downstairs and found Asa and Simon helping Martha bring in vegetables for supper.

"I was afraid that he was getting worse," Asa said. "If he rests, he can recover."

Martha nodded as Mary came down from Lazarus's room. "Sister, we will look in on Lazarus in a little while. For now, we need to take care of our guest."

Simon shook his head. "I am under your roof as a guest, but our Lord did not heal my disease so that I could have a week of rest. I am your servant."

Martha scoffed. "You are no servant."

Mary led the others into the house. "Simon, we are glad to have you here in our home. You must let us serve you."

She watched as Simon handed his basket to Martha. He seemed to have a smile forming at the corners of his eyes.

"I am a servant of Jesus. I owe him everything," Simon said. "I will go where he sends me, and I will do what needs to be done."

Martha tilted her head toward him. "We appreciate your willingness to help."

"May I ask a question?" Simon quickly added, "It is personal, and you do not have to answer."

Mary listened carefully. She knew that Martha didn't usually like personal questions.

"I will answer if I can," Martha replied.

Simon seemed to study Martha's face and her hands, especially her scars. "Jesus healed your sister, and he healed me. Hordes of people follow him all the time, asking for healing. Why have you not asked?"

Mary held her breath, waiting for Martha to respond. She had wanted to ask the same question but never found the right words.

"I have thought about it," Martha said. "I have. But when Jesus heals, when he has performed any miracle, it has been because the receivers had a great need. Your body was dying. Mary's mind was dying. The blind and lame and hungry have such great need." She stretched out her arm and pulled her veil back, completely exposing her scars for Simon to see, almost as a challenge.

He didn't flinch or look away.

"My scars do not cause me pain. They do not keep me from my work. They are just ugly."

Simon looked Martha in the eye and smiled. "Everything that is a part of you is beautiful. You are quite right. You do not need healing."

Simon's words seemed to startle Martha. Mary watched as her sister's face flushed a bright pink.

Asa and Mary exchanged a glance, almost embarrassed to be witnesses to such a tender moment. "Well, Lazarus will be well and back in the fields soon," Asa said.

Mary knew that he was hoping to redirect the conversation. "Until then, he knows that you will take care of the crops for Jeb and him. You are a good foreman."

Asa picked up the clay jar at the door. "I will fetch water for the evening and bring Vera in from the garden."

Mary and Martha prepared supper while Simon offered prayers on the portico for Lazarus.

They had just finished setting the table when Vera and Asa came running inside.

"What is it?" Mary and Simon asked at the same time. Vera had tears in her eyes.

"There were travelers at the well. They told me that Jesus and his followers had angered some of the religious leaders in Jerusalem," Asa explained. "Some tried to stone him."

Simon shook his head. "What happened? Was anyone hurt?"

Asa shrugged. "They could not tell me anything but that Jesus disappeared." He shook his head. "They said that he was not stoned, but that His enemies would not let him slip away next time."

Vera swallowed hard. "It is like with the John the Baptizer. He crossed a powerful man, and he was imprisoned and executed. I cannot bear the thought of Jesus being taken."

Martha raised her hand to her lips. Mary put her arm around Vera's shoulder. "It will be all right, Vera."

The young girl wiped her face with the back of her hand. "John baptized Josiah and me. He was bold and kind. He told us that Jesus would make everything right. Still, they killed John. What will they do to Jesus?"

Mary's heart slammed against her ribs. She could see a cloud of worry settle over everyone's expressions. She recognized the fear; she knew it well. "We cannot fall away now. Jesus will be all right."

Simon nodded. He gestured to the table. "We should pray. We should pray for Jesus and his men. We should pray for us all."

CHAPTER

TWENTY-ONE

The next week was better for Lazarus, and Mary felt relieved to see her brother back in the fields working. When the Sabbath was over, Simon went back to his home on the other side of Bethany. Simon had told them how anxious he was to see his mother and father again.

Martha and Mary visited him a few days later with a basket of fresh vegetables from the garden. His parents seemed overwhelmed with joy to have their son back. They told Mary that they had spent the last few years mourning him, sure that they would never again see him alive.

After leaving Simon's house, the sisters took another bundle of linens and food to the hospice. Again, the nurse took the parcels from their hands and disappeared behind the door.

"I just wish I could see that they were going to be used," Martha said.

Mary nodded. "I understand. I hate to think that they are being stacked somewhere."

Vera laughed. "If the nurse takes them from you, she will use them."

Mary tilted her head and shrugged her shoulders. "How can you be sure?"

Vera lowered her chin, "I cannot be sure, of course. But I do not believe that she would take them just for the sake of appearances. That would make more work for her and for the other nurses there."

Martha raised her brow. "Perhaps, but I wish I could go inside and see."

Vera shook her head. "I think they close the door so quickly because they are trying to keep you safe from the illnesses inside."

Mary exchanged a glance with Martha. "Of course, sister," she said. "And we do not ask to come in. They probably just want to protect us."

Martha nodded. "I suppose this is not an occasion to host friends."

"Vera is right," Mary said. "We should be content knowing that they have accepted our gifts. They are gifts, after all, to be used as they like."

The women went to Bethany's market to purchase more wool and some fish for supper. It seemed that everywhere they went people were talking about Jesus and his men. Miracles in Galilee. Great sermons on this hillside or that shoreline. People healed of every imaginable disease. Even a few rumors of a boy being raised from the dead.

Mary wondered at everything she heard. She didn't doubt that any of it was true, but she still was amazed. And for every miraculous sign, there were other rumors, too. The murmurs that Jesus was planning to overthrow Herod, or Caesar, or one of the many other leaders in this city or that.

Mary had listened to her friend speak of a great kingdom that was to come, but Jesus had never mentioned any desire to live in a palace or rule over the citizens of Jerusalem, Rome, or anywhere for that matter. She knew he only talked about other people as his brothers and sisters. He told her many times that he had come to serve, not to be served. None of that sounded like a man plotting his political ambitions.

She offered a quick prayer for Jesus' safety and the protection of his followers. Martha had finished her shopping and was turning to go home when they heard a shopkeeper talking to another customer. "Yes, they said he considered himself equal to God. Many wish him dead for such blasphemy. They intended to stone him in the Temple."

Mary froze in her steps. Martha clutched Mary's arm and squeezed. Mary was afraid that Martha might faint. They listened for more news.

"I have heard that he has healed many. That there are hundreds of witnesses," the businessman said.

"Some say he heals by the power of the devil," the customer replied. "I could not say, but some from the council say that they must deal with him soon."

Mary couldn't hear anything but her own breathing, and soon the air around her became thick and stale. She didn't know if she was holding Martha or if Martha was holding her. She wanted to ask the man for more information but didn't dare. Vera kept her head and approached the men with a low bow.

"Forgive me," she whispered. "My mistresses could not help but hear that you spoke of a man."

The shopkeeper nodded. "I did not mean to distress your mistresses."

Vera shook her head and continued. "Please, sir, can you tell me of whom you were speaking?"

The customer knit his brow and exhaled. Mary leaned in to hear.

"The man is Jesus of Nazareth." The man glanced at Mary and Martha, then back to Vera. "He has not been stoned, yet. Did you ever hear of him?"

A flood of tears rushed over Vera's cheeks, and she nodded as she turned back to Mary. "Yes. Thank you," she said to the man through sobs.

Martha wrapped her arm around Vera's shoulders. "Let us go home," she said. Her voice sounded thick with emotion.

Mary walked with Martha and Vera back to the house. They didn't speak but instead cried. Mary felt a mixture of relief that neither Jesus nor his men had been harmed, as well as overwhelming sorrow for them. She knew that Jesus offered a message of love and forgiveness. In turn, his listeners offered death. A wave of grief swept over her.

Once they reached the house, they prepared supper with only quiet murmurs when necessary. Mary wondered if Martha intended to tell Lazarus, and if so, then how?

Vera's tears had dried, but she continued to sniff for another hour. Mary couldn't think of anything to say that might comfort her. She reached out her hand and patted Vera's arm a few times. It seemed insignificant, but each time she did it, Vera responded with a weak smile.

When Lazarus finally returned with Asa for the night, Mary could see that they had already heard the news. The men's eyes looked red and swollen, and their faces appeared fatigued.

After the blessing, they all ate their supper with few words. As Mary helped Vera clear the table, Lazarus leaned back and looked at the ceiling. "Almighty Yahweh, we beg your mercy. We have suffered significant loss as a family, and now we fear for the safety of our beloved friends."

They spent the rest of the evening in prayer, and Mary wished that Jesus was near. She wanted to let him know that they were praying for them. At the same time, she hoped that he was far away from the perils of Herod's whims and safe in the home of another friend. Perhaps he was already in the Decapolis.

Mary listened as Martha sang one of the psalms their mother used to sing when she was sad. Everything else was quiet, and for a moment, Mary thought that perhaps the whole world was listening to Martha's song.

As she stretched out on her bed, Mary felt grateful for all that she had. She thanked God for her home, and for all that Tirzah had given them. She was thankful for Vera and Josiah and Asa. For the work that they had. For the opportunities to share with others. She thanked God for Jesus and for his message. Most of all she was grateful for Martha and for Lazarus.

"Oh Lord," she whispered. "What would I do without Martha and Lazarus?"

CHAPTER

TWENTY-TWO

Mary awoke to the sound of Lazarus's coughing. She looked across the room toward her sister, who sat straight up in her bed as well. Another rumbling cough rolled through the house. The women hurried into the other room, barely noticing that it was still dark outside. Lazarus sat in a chair by the oil lamp sipping at a cup of water.

"I apologize for waking you," he whispered.

Mary wondered if he was trying to keep quiet, or if his voice had no more strength.

"Let us help you," Martha said. She pointed to one of the blankets near the door. "Mary, wrap a blanket around his shoulders. I have some herbs to make a poultice for his throat."

Mary draped the blanket over her brother's back. She could see his hands trembling in the lamplight. His skin felt warm, but she could see him shivering.

"Brother, you have taken ill again," she said. "You must rest."

"I must do a great many things," he said in short rasps. "Much to do, and little time for it all."

Mary felt concern grow in her heart as Lazarus's words lingered. "You should not speak like that. You have a cough. You will recover soon." She looked at Martha with worry in her eyes.

"If you get enough rest, you will be well," Martha said.

"You always tell me to rest," Lazarus said, finishing with another fit of wheezing. "You speak to me as one speaks to a grandfather. I am your brother. I am ill. It grows worse every day, not better. Soon all I will do is rest."

Mary felt tears forming. She knelt at her brother's side. "You will be all right. Jesus will come back soon. He can help."

Lazarus shook his head. "He should not come back to Jerusalem or Bethany. It is far too dangerous for him."

Martha placed a cup of hot broth in his hands and began chopping the ingredients for her remedy. "It is dangerous for him. Things have gotten worse, it is true. But you are his friend. He will come for you."

"Perhaps, but he could not even save John the Baptist," Lazarus said. As his cough returned, he struggled to steady the cup without spilling the broth.

Mary bit her lip and tried not to think about her brother's words. *Jesus could have saved John*, she thought silently. *But he did not.*

The harder she tried to blot out the thought from her mind, the bigger it became. She felt a knot forming in her stomach. She knew that Jesus could heal her brother. He had restored her with just a word and a touch. She had watched him heal Simon from certain death. Lazarus just had a cough. It would be easy for Jesus.

She looked at her brother, her worries spinning in a haze of confusion. Lazarus coughed again. Mary's thoughts came into sharp focus as she noticed something on his hand after his wheezing. It was blood.

Martha seemed to see it at the same time, and Lazarus saw a few seconds later. He tried to wipe the red away before the women noticed.

"How long have you been coughing blood?" Martha asked.

Mary stood and took hold of Lazarus's shoulder. She felt a shiver run through him.

"I cannot say for sure." His voice faded into a cough, and Lazarus struggled just to breathe.

"Josiah! Asa!" Martha cried out the window.

Mary shook her head and wondered what to do. Lazarus's condition was worse than she expected. Worse than any of them knew.

Mary paced for a minute and then reached up for her box of oil on the shelf. "I will take this to Bethany and bring back a physician."

"No," Martha and Lazarus said together.

While Lazarus punctuated his protest with more coughing, Martha only shook her head and snatched the box from Mary's hands. After placing the oil back on the shelf, she leaned close to Mary's ear. "If anything happens to our brother, that oil will be all that we have left," she whispered.

"We cannot spend it on doctors and remedies that may not help."

"He is our brother," Mary pleaded.

"I know that," Martha said. "I know." She bit her lip and turned away quickly. She looked out the window and then back to Mary. "Go find one of the men. We will tell Jesus about our brother."

Mary hurried outside into the fresh early morning. Though the sky was still dark, a growing purple light was forming over the hills to the east. Mary walked toward it, desperate for help.

She saw a shadow in front of her and recognized the silhouette as Asa. "Come quickly," she cried. "Lazarus is worse."

"I was concerned about him yesterday," he answered. They rushed back to the house side-by-side.

"He woke us with his coughing," she explained. "There was blood."

She could almost feel Asa slowing his pace as they reached the portico. "If there is blood, what can we do?"

"I know, but Martha wants to send word to Jesus. He can help." Mary nodded, hoping to convince herself as well as Asa.

"I believe he could help," he said in a hushed tone, "if he were here."

They entered the house to find Martha helping Lazarus into Mary's bed. She could see him shaking with chills though he was already wrapped in blankets.

"He is too weak to climb stairs," Martha started to explain as if she expected Mary to resist.

"Of course, he should have my bed. You must take care of him," Mary said with a nod. "I will help Asa get a message together for Jesus."

Martha continued to fret over her brother as if she couldn't hear anything but his cough.

Mary could see the despair in Asa's expression. "I will send my most trusted man. There is talk that Jesus is at the Jordan, where John preached. He can be there in a day or so." Asa murmured a prayer under his breath. "Peter told me that Jesus once healed a man with just a word from a great distance. Perhaps he will do the same now."

Mary stared at Asa and struggled to push a question through her lips. "Will Lazarus last that long?" she finally whispered.

Asa took a deep breath and turned from her. "I will send him before dawn," he said over his shoulder. "Pray."

TWENTY-THREE

Tears filled the whole day. Lazarus slept when he wasn't coughing. Martha stayed busy making poultices and broths, and Mary kept vigil at Lazarus's side. Asa spent hours traveling between the fields, the house, and the market, trying to do the work of three men.

Vera and Josiah searched for a physician in Bethany willing to help, but once Lazarus's symptoms were made known, they only shook their heads and offered condolences. Josiah even made the journey to Jerusalem, but there was no willing doctor there, either. He stopped to see Tirzah, hoping she might have something for comfort, but the ointment she sent made no difference in Lazarus's condition.

"What else can we do?" Martha asked Mary as the sun descended behind the hills. "We have tried every remedy, and our brother is no better than he was this morning."

"If Jesus comes right away, Lazarus will be healed," Mary said.

"I do not doubt," Martha replied. She looked out the window as the sky began to turn a pale lavender color. "But our Lord is still two days' away, including his journey back here."

"We will pray for healing for our brother and faith for ourselves," Mary whispered.

A knock on the door startled the women, and they jumped. Vera gasped and hopped to her feet as Mary opened the door.

Tirzah and a young servant boy stood in the deepening twilight. Without a word, Mary threw her arms around her friend and began to sob.

Martha wiped her damp cheeks and motioned for everyone to move inside. "Dear sister, you should not have traveled the Jericho road so late in the day. You might have been overtaken by thieves."

"The Lord protects," Tirzah said. She uttered a short blessing over the house as she crossed the threshold. "Has my salve helped at all?" she asked.

She was answered by a low rumbling cough by Lazarus. She shook her head and pulled off her wrap. She nodded to Mary and Martha with a look of despair in her eyes.

"He is very ill," Mary said. "If he gets more rest," she began, but her brother's wheezing interrupted her.

"May I offer you both some water after your journey?" Martha asked as Vera reached for the pitcher.

Tirzah knit her brows and frowned. "My dear friend, I am

not a guest. I am here to serve your family. I want to be of help."

At that, Martha's tears flooded her face, and she fell into Tirzah's arms. "You are too good to us."

"Your family is precious to me in ways that I cannot explain. You are part of me as if I had birthed you myself. You are the daughters God gave to me in my darkest time. He used a terrible act of my own child to bring a light into my life. I will do whatever I can to help you now."

Vera lit another lamp on the table, and Tirzah's servant unpacked a basket carrying food and oil. Martha went to Lazarus's side as he again coughed and sputtered. Vera hurried to her with a basin to clean away the blood.

"You sent word to Jesus?" Tirzah asked.

"Asa's messenger left at sunrise. He believed Jesus to be at the Jordan near Bethabara," Mary explained.

"That is what I heard, too." Tirzah clutched her small hands together and sighed. "Jesus will come."

"He will," Mary agreed.

When Martha returned to the table, the older woman studied her face and then turned to Mary. "You both have been at your brother's side all day?"

"Yes," Martha said as Mary nodded.

"And Vera, too, I suppose?"

"Yes."

"Let Eustace and I watch over Lazarus for a few hours. You three must get some rest." Tirzah didn't wait for permission. She only stood and went to the bedroom door, rolling up her sleeves as she walked.

Martha tried to resist, but Tirzah preempted her protest.

"You are all resilient women; your brother needs you to be strong. If you let yourself catch his cough, he will be angry with you."

Mary chewed on her lip. Her body ached for sleep, but she knew that she couldn't possibly rest tonight. Her fears were too big. Her worries were too big. Her brother was too weak.

"Our God created this whole world and everything in it," Martha whispered as if she had heard Mary's thoughts. "Jesus will ask God to heal our brother, and he will."

Mary felt like melting into a pool of tears, but she was too exhausted to cry. "We will try to rest," she said.

"All three of you should eat something and then go upstairs and sleep. I will wake you if needed," Tirzah instructed.

Eustace served the women some stew and bread, and they ate their small supper in silence.

After a few minutes, Mary noticed. "Lazarus has not coughed since we began to eat. Perhaps he is getting better," she said.

Martha nodded. "We should sleep for a little while. It will be difficult, but tomorrow will be worse if we cannot work."

Eustace handed Vera a lamp, and they hurried upstairs to prepare the room while Martha and Mary cleaned up the table. When they were done, they went into the bedroom for a few minutes to see their brother.

"Lazarus," Mary whispered, not wanting to stir him. She leaned close to his chest and listened. He breathed slowly, and it sounded like his breath was bubbling through a fountain. She pressed her eyes closed and prayed. "Yahweh Rapha, heal and restore him."

Mary watched as Martha did the same. Listening. Praying. Hoping. That was all they could do for now.

Eustace came back and handed them each a lamp to light the stairs. "I will not sleep tonight," he assured them. "Your brother will lack for nothing."

Mary followed Martha up to the bedroom where they discovered that Vera had arranged two pallets on the floor. Martha stretched out on Lazarus's bed, and Mary and Vera curled up on their blankets. Mary watched as Vera drifted off to sleep first, and then Martha quickly after. Mary gazed for a few minutes at the stars out the window.

"Jesus, please come back," she said through a yawn. The stars seemed to fade one by one into a black pool of wishes and tears.

CHAPTER

TWENTY-FOUR

All three women bolted straight upright from their sleep at the same moment. The house was silent as they listened for whatever sound woke them. Nothing.

They all quickly brushed through their hair with their fingers and hurried down to see how Lazarus was. The sun was not yet burning but cast a pink hue on the horizon. Mary smiled for a moment as she felt a shiver run up her spine. She pulled open the door, and Martha and Vera rushed past her.

Eustace stood over the fire, stirring a broth. Tirzah leaned over Lazarus and chanted a prayer that Mary remembered hearing her mother sing years ago.

"How is he?" Martha asked. "We did not hear any coughing all night."

Tirzah motioned for them to come close. "His cough is gone, and I was hopeful," she began. She took their hands and kissed them. "But this morning his breathing has slowed. It is difficult for him. His life is fading."

Mary shook her head. "Our messenger should reach Jesus today. He will heal him from afar. He has done that before."

Tirzah nodded. "He may still save him, beloved. But you must prepare yourself and give Lazarus your blessing."

Martha's chin began to quiver, and she pressed her lips into a thin, tight line. "Is it not for him to leave us with a blessing?" she asked.

Though Martha's words sounded bitter, Mary knew that Martha wanted nothing more than to hear her brother's voice one more time.

Tirzah nodded. "It is. But your sweet Lazarus has nothing left to offer."

Mary's heart felt as though it were tearing in half. She knelt at Lazarus's side and began to pray again. "I exalt You, Lord, for you have uplifted me, and did not allow my enemies to rejoice over me. Lord, my God, I cried out to You, and You healed me. Lord, You have brought up my soul from the grave; You have kept me alive, that I should not descend to the pit." She paused her psalm as a tremor passed through Lazarus's body.

He drew a shallow breath and looked as though he would cough, but as his face strained to force the air out, only a gurgling sound came. Martha, Vera, and Tirzah dropped to their knees beside Mary, and Eustace stood in the doorway, watching.

Lazarus sucked in another tiny swallow of air, but

couldn't push it back out. His tortured face strained one last time and then relaxed slightly. He was gone.

Martha's head dropped onto his chest, and she began to moan. Vera and Tirzah's sobs became an echo of the aches and groans of Martha. Mary allowed her tears to fall, but she wrestled with herself. Her beloved brother was dead, and her heart was pierced with disappointment.

Jesus had not come.

CHAPTER

TWENTY-FIVE

Mourners filled the little house on the edge of Bethany. Wailing and moaning flooded the air. Friends brought baskets of food. Tirzah helped Martha prepare for the burial. Mary helped where she could, but mostly she sat and watched.

As the sun rose high overhead, she calculated how long it might be until Jesus got the news that Lazarus was ill. *Maybe even still. . .* She dared to wish. But as the day wore on, her hope wore away with it. *Surely, he has heard by now, and perhaps there was nothing to be done.*

Her heart ached. She wanted to talk to Lazarus. He would tell her to be strong and wait. But he couldn't. She cried, but she was too weary to mourn properly. The wailing would go on without her.

She sat in the garden for a little while. A part of her watched the horizon, hoping. As evening approached, she wandered inside to help Martha prepare supper, but she found that her sister had ceded her post in the kitchen to Tirzah's household servants. Tirzah chirped orders to one and then another, and Martha sat on a stool next to where Lazarus lay.

All their friends came to weep with them. It was the same people who had cried at their sides when their mother and father had died. Mary thought to herself about how she had not seen most of them since her parents' deaths. She nodded as they offered prayers and tears.

Darkness enfolded the house and friends went home. The mourners softened their wails. Mary and Martha sat at the table and stared at each other over the struggling lamp.

Mary noticed how empty Martha's eyes looked. Her complexion seemed gray and dull, and her lips were drawn thin and chapped. Mary wondered if she appeared the same. Had they welcomed all of Bethany and half of Jerusalem to their home looking like withered grass? Did it matter? Their most important guest never came.

"Bring it all inside," Tirzah instructed as Asa carried a large basket from the portico. She turned to the sisters. "I spoke with one of your brother's dear friends, Nicodemus, and he will be here before sunset to help us carry Lazarus to the tomb."

Mary watched as Martha's eyes blinked slowly. It was the only indication that Martha heard Tirzah's words.

"Nicodemus is a good man," Mary said. The sound of her own voice startled her, and a shiver run down her spine.

"Yes," Tirzah said. Vera and Asa began to empty the

basket's contents onto the table and the other bed. "We have all of the spices we need and the wrappings."

Mary knew Tirzah was asking them to join her in preparing Lazarus's body. She resisted. She still wanted to believe. *She needed to believe.* How could she have faith in a man who had failed her so completely?

"How is this possible?" Martha said.

Mary studied her sister's exhausted face. She heard the words, but there was no hint that Martha had actually spoken them. Martha hadn't moved a fraction of an inch.

"This is the way of death and of life," Tirzah answered. "The soul is given to us for a while and then returns to the Creator's hand."

"If he had been here," Martha said. Her voice faltered, and her chin dropped. "If I had sent for him sooner, maybe?"

Mary shook her head and reached out for Martha's hand. "You cannot blame yourself. Neither of us knew how sick our brother was. He concealed it from us until it was too late."

"And now you blame Lazarus?" Martha accused. Her voice strengthened, and she drew her hand back from Mary's.

"No, of course, I do not blame him," Mary pleaded. "I should have gone for a physician a week ago. This is my fault."

Tirzah clicked her tongue and glared. "You both must hush now," she said.

Mary recognized the tone as one their mother often took when they would argue as children. She nodded and stretched out her hands palms up, in surrender to her sister's anger. "I am so sorry."

"You are tired. Both of you," Tirzah said. "You are hurting so much that you forget how terribly everyone else is hurting."

Mary's eyes filled with tears and she began to tremble.

"You still have each other. You must cling to one another in times like these," Tirzah whispered.

Mary's anger and resentment and sorrow and hope all crumbled into one giant landslide of emotion. She fell to her knees and dropped her head into her sister's lap. "Oh, Martha! How can he be gone? He was everything to our family. Who will protect us now? Who will care for us? We have lost everything."

And with that, Mary's real mourning began. Martha sobbed over her. Vera and Tirzah cried as they organized the burial clothes and spices. Asa left the women to their tears.

An hour passed before Mary's weeping subsided. She sat back on the floor and clutched Martha's scarred hand. She drew slow breaths and became aware of the deep ache in her bones.

She kissed Martha's hands. "Sister, you are my greatest treasure. I cannot say what tomorrow brings, but I will meet it with your strength and courage at my side."

Martha wiped at Mary's cheeks with her thumbs. "You are the one with courage."

Tirzah stepped back into the room with them. "We have everything ready."

Mary still didn't want to cover her brother's body with myrrh and spices or wrap him in linen. She didn't want to pray or sing or cry over him. She wanted only to talk to him again.

Martha helped raise Mary to her feet. She hugged her shoulder and whispered in her ear. "I can only face this because I have you with me."

Mary needed to hear just those words at just that moment. "We have each other," she replied.

TWENTY-SIX

Mary and Martha followed behind as Asa and Nicodemus carried Lazarus's body to the cart. The donkey allowed the men to hitch him without protest, and the long walk to the tomb began.

Tirzah and Vera fell into the procession behind the sisters, followed by the mourners, and then the family friends. All along the path to the garden, the people of Bethany stopped in their tracks as the body of Lazarus passed. They waited for everyone, showing respect for the dead, and then went back to their work. A few fell into line and joined in the march.

At the top of the hill, the cart slowed to a stop. Asa and Nicodemus gently carried their friend down the steep path to the small cave cut into the earth. Mary held tight to her sister's hand, not wanting to take the first step into the garden. She looked around at all the faces. Friends. Mourners. Everyone weeping dutifully. Everyone loved Lazarus.

She searched for another face, but it wasn't there.

Why not? Where are you?

Martha shook her head as if she heard Mary's questions.

Tirzah nudged them on. "We must go down to the tomb now."

Mary drew a deep breath and clung to Martha. The rocky steps were well-worn with use. As the women walked, they kept their eyes down, avoiding the sight of the yawning black opening of their family tomb.

But at the base of the steps, it was in front of them, a gaping mouth forming the silent scream of Mary's pain, frozen into the rock. Nicodemus prayed over Lazarus. Mary and Martha whispered their goodbyes as they walked into the dark cave after the men.

Martha waited as Lazarus was gently placed on the stone shelf. She recited her prayer as she opened her pouch of herbs and resins and began tucking the myrrh and lavender into the folds of the burial linens.

Mary watched her sister and listened to the prayer. She tried to pray with her, but Mary struggled to focus on the words. All she could hear was the plea from her heart.

Jesus, please come.

Nicodemus faced the women as Asa nodded and joined the others outside.

Mary met his gaze and then quickly looked away. "I cannot leave him yet."

Martha rested her hands on Mary's shoulders. "Nicodemus must get back to Jerusalem. He has obligations."

"I cannot leave Lazarus yet," Mary repeated.

Nicodemus nodded to Martha. "There is no hurry."

Martha lowered her chin and seemed to continue her prayer. Mary just stood at Lazarus's side. She couldn't pray. She couldn't touch her brother. She couldn't look at her sister. She couldn't bring herself to look up at all.

Mary could feel time passing, slipping away from them all. She could feel the cold of the ground seeping into her bones. Martha and Nicodemus were growing impatient with her; she knew it without a glance or sound from them. Another shiver gripped her and shook her whole body.

"Perhaps we should go out now," Nicodemus whispered.

Martha didn't wait for a reply. She took Mary's arm in her grasp and led her back into the garden.

Nicodemus kissed both women on each cheek and then turned to begin his climb up the steps. Asa and a few other men started to roll the tombstone into place.

"Wait," Mary said. She thought she was shouting, but her voice was nothing more than a whisper, and the massive stone came to rest.

Mary sank to her knees. Martha left her there to go speak to Tirzah and the mourners. Most of the other people had already gone home.

Mary cried. Jesus wasn't there, and Lazarus was dead. Mary could think of nothing else.

You did not come. We needed you, and you did not come.

And now it was too late.

CHAPTER

TWENTY-SEVEN

The house was empty without Lazarus. Mary sat, or stood, or walked in a shell. *I have no purpose,* she thought to herself. She still was afraid to listen to her own thoughts; afraid they might well up again and take over her mind. Instead, she focused on her surroundings.

Every sound seemed to ring off the walls. The mourners continued to wail. The fire crackled. The wind blew and rattled the shuttered windows.

Martha didn't speak. Tirzah had kissed them goodbye and left after the burial. Her husband and son were returning home, and she needed to be there when they arrived.

The sun set and rose again. Mary ate, slept, mourned. Everything had changed, but it was all the same. Vera and Asa worked quietly. They needed no oversight.

Two days, maybe three, had passed. Mary could take it no longer. Everything was too loud and too quiet at the same time. She had to get out of the house, so she picked up the water jar and walked toward the door.

"I will go with you," Vera said.

"I can fetch the water myself." Mary didn't make eye contact with anyone.

Martha shook her head and motioned for Vera to follow.

"I need to walk, too," Vera replied, and followed behind Mary.

Mary sighed and shrugged, staring straight ahead as she stepped into the bright sunlight. She walked to the well with a slow but steady gait. Mary didn't look around or speak. She paid no attention to Vera. She just walked.

When they reached the well, Vera took the water jar from Mary without asking. She drew the water while Mary sat on the short stone wall nearby.

Mary's heart began to pound. She finally opened her eyes. She was sitting in the same place where her attacker had been. Where she had served him just before he raped her. Where her world had changed forever.

She gasped for air and looked into the clear blue sky. "Where are you, Lord?" she prayed.

"Yahweh is here." Vera's voice startled Mary.

She hadn't realized that her plea had made a sound at all. It took several seconds for Mary to understand that she had spoken and Vera replied.

"What?"

Vera placed the water jar on the ground and took a seat beside her friend. "Yahweh is here with us, always. Even when it seems he is far away, he is with us."

Mary swallowed hard. This was not what she wanted to

hear. Vera didn't know what Mary was feeling. She certainly didn't know what she needed most. She needed Jesus to be here. She knew it was too late for Lazarus, but somehow, she needed him for herself. She felt like crying, but her eyes were dry. She had an anger flickering in her belly, and she didn't want to admit it.

"You cannot know what I feel," she began.

"I know. I could never really understand what you have gone through. What you are feeling right now." Vera took her hand. "I am blessed by the Almighty to have you and your sister. I was blessed to know your brother."

Mary wanted to pull away and run back home, but she didn't. She listened.

"Jesus will come back here. He loved your brother. He loves you and Martha, too. Until He returns, you must wait and hope." Vera leaned her head against Mary's shoulder.

"What hope?" Mary whispered. There were dozens more things she wanted to say. She wanted to shout and scream. How could they hope for anything more than a life of poverty and disgrace? They had no chance for marriage. They had no prospects of support. Mary knew that their only chance of survival was to ask their nearest relative to take their land and home and them in the bargain. Damaged merchandise, the whole lot.

"There is always hope," Vera said. She sat up straight and looked Mary in the eye.

Mary shook her head. "We have lost too much. I want to hope," she said, "but even if Jesus returned today, what could He do?"

"He saved you. He saved your mind," Vera reminded her.

"He saved much more than that." Mary allowed herself think for a moment of the awful things that had taken over her heart and mind. She knew that Jesus' touch had rescued her from a darkness she still couldn't fathom.

"But would he not save you again?"

Mary stared back at the girl wondering if she understood the magnitude of the situation. Vera had always been cared for, living in a comfortable house with Tirzah. Mary put her hand to Vera's cheek and thought of what to do with the sweet soul in front of her.

"I wish it were as simple as that," Mary said. "Martha and I have no relatives nearby. We may convince a cousin to take our property, and perhaps allow us to stay, but that is not a certainty. The Romans have brought Israel more opportunities for women, but our Jewish traditions do not permit too many freedoms."

Vera nodded. "You have suffered a great sorrow. Both you and Martha have endured terrible pains. But Jesus speaks of a kingdom. In his kingdom, surely there will be even more opportunity, and you and your sister are favored by him."

"He does speak of a kingdom," Mary said with a deep sigh. Her mind wandered back to the first time she sat at Jesus' feet and listened to him talk. "I know this kingdom is real, but I think somehow it is more than a throne in Jerusalem. I cannot explain it, but his words have a deeper message than that. Jesus is bigger than Caiaphas, or Pilate, or even Caesar himself. He is from the Almighty God. He is more that that."

Vera raised her brows and allowed a slight smile to frame her lips. "You do have hope."

Mary took the girl's hands and stood. When she did, it was like a heavy weight fell off of her shoulders. She filled her lungs with fresh air. She picked up the water jar and turned her face to the sun. Warmth.

"I have not felt warm since we buried my brother."

Vera reached out and again took the water jar without asking. "You and Martha are good women, but you both forget how much you need each other. In another day, the mourners will leave, and it will just be the two of you. You need to lean on each other. You need to talk to each other."

Mary looked at this young girl, wise beyond her years, and a tear finally escaped her eyes. Perhaps she did understand that they had nothing. Nothing but each other.

Vera turned quickly and led the way back home. After just a few steps, she looked over her shoulder to Mary. "And you have me, and I need you both, too."

Mary followed Vera back to the house. She thought about how blessed she was to have Martha, and that she really should make more of an effort to understand her. Mary ached for all the loss they both had suffered, but she couldn't imagine spending the rest of her life in the painful quiet they had shared these last few days. She had to find hope, and soon.

As the house came into view, Mary realized that the mourners had quieted somewhat. Vera must have noticed it, too, because she cast a confused glance back to Mary. They went inside to find Martha gone. Vera sat the water jar down and hurried to the front of the house

"Where is my sister?" Mary asked one of the few mourners still wailing at the door.

"She was called away just after you left to fetch water."

Vera came back inside after speaking to a young boy on the portico. "They said she was going out to the tomb." She poured a cup of water for Mary. "She will return soon, I believe."

Mary waited at the table, trying hard to drown out the sound of the wailing all around her. The mourners were few, but they seemed more determined than ever to fill the house with their moans.

"I feel cold again," Mary whispered to Vera. She walked to the window and pulled open the shutters. A burst of sunlight flooded the room and softened the cries of the mourners.

In the distance, she could see Martha approaching. She took a deep breath. Martha had gone to the grave without her. Perhaps she was angry. Maybe she thought Mary didn't understand. Maybe she didn't.

She clutched at the window sill as if she would fall to the floor if she let go. Her fingers pressed hard into the wood frame. She felt anxious, unsure of what Martha might say to her if she spoke at all. But when Martha came closer, she saw something in her expression had changed.

Martha rushed inside and took Mary by both hands.

"What is it, sister?" Mary asked as Martha gasped for breath.

"He is here. The Messiah is here, and he is asking for you."

Mary didn't need any more explanation. She squeezed her sister's hand, and together they hurried to the edge of the garden. The rest of the mourners followed after them.

Reaching the edge of the garden, she saw a large crowd gathered. She searched for her friend's face. When she finally caught sight of Jesus, she began to run. Tears streamed down her face. She left her sister behind, and she ran to Jesus, crying. When she reached him, she fell at his feet. "Teacher, if you had been here, Lazarus would not have died. I know you could have healed him."

As he had once before, Jesus reached out to take Mary's hand and lift her to her feet. "Where is your brother?" he asked.

Martha joined them and motioned to the sealed tomb, and Mary led him to the steps down into the garden. "He is buried here," she said. "Come see."

Jesus followed the women down the stone steps to the graveside.

Mary placed her hands on the giant stone resting over the mouth of the cave. The stone felt warm to the touch from the day's sun. "He is in here." When she turned to face Jesus, she could see the tears rolling over his cheeks. Her heart ached all over again.

"My brother loved you," Martha said to Jesus.

Jesus nodded. "And I him," he said and wiped back the tears. "Take the stone away," he instructed the men standing nearby.

Martha held up her hands to stop them. "No, Master, he has been entombed for four days now. By this time, there will be a terrible odor."

Mary agreed. "Oh no, Teacher."

"I have told you both," Jesus said, "if you believe you will see God's glory."

Mary looked at Martha and nodded. "Please," she whispered. She knew that Jesus needed to see his friend one more time.

Martha gestured to the men. "Do as he says."

As the men pulled back the stone, Jesus looked up to the sky and began to pray. Mary listened as he thanked Yahweh for hearing his request. Her heart pounded in her ears as she realized what he was saying. He did not want to enter the tomb of a dead man. This was something more.

Before she could imagine what would happen next, she heard Jesus call, "Lazarus, come out!"

Mary couldn't think. She couldn't move. Martha reached out and grabbed her hand, and the women steadied themselves against each other. A great silence enveloped the whole crowd as everyone seemed to hold their collective breath.

A few seconds later it happened. Mary's brother stepped into the sunlight, still wrapped in the linen grave clothes. Martha gasped in shock and ran to his side, and Mary dropped to her knees.

"Get up, Mary, and help your sister remove Lazarus's burial linens." Jesus helped her back to her feet and took her to her brother.

"Jesus saved you," she heard Martha saying as they tugged the wrappings from Lazarus's head and face.

"My sisters." Lazarus embraced the women and reached out to Jesus. "My friend."

Jesus wrapped his arms around the reunited family and wept with them for several minutes.

"Lord, you are the Messiah," Martha said. "Mary believed

this from the moment she knew you. I was slow to trust, but I know it's true now."

Lazarus held his sisters close. "The Messiah is here!" he cried out for all to hear. "Yahweh is with us!"

Mary didn't even try to hide her tears. She reached out to take Jesus' hand. "You must come to our home," she insisted. "You and everyone with you."

Martha nodded. "Yes, and you shall stay with us all as long as you are here."

Jesus walked with them back up the stairs and to the road leading home. He motioned to his traveling companions. "We will stay with you for the night," he agreed, "but we must leave tomorrow. You all need some time together without a crowd of people to feed."

Mary couldn't contain her smile. She felt as though she hadn't smiled in months, and now her face would do nothing else.

Martha and Vera sent home the mourners, and for the first time in a week, their house was filled to the roof with joy.

After supper, everyone gathered on the portico to listen and to talk with Jesus. He told them about his travels, and about the moment when he was told that Lazarus was sick, and his trip back to Bethany.

"Will you reconsider about leaving us tomorrow?" Mary asked. "It is no trouble at all to feed you."

Jesus patted her hand and smiled. "Your family is dear to me. But you know that trouble is near wherever I go now. Word of what I did for your brother has already reached Jerusalem."

Mary clutched his hand. "I am frightened for you. For all of you."

Jesus shook his head. "Do not fear for me. You have glimpsed the glory of God today, but you will see much more."

"When Lazarus died," she whispered, "I was afraid we would never see you again. I cannot bear the thought of that."

Jesus leaned close to Mary's ear. "You will see me again, dear sister."

His words still echoed in her ears long after she kissed her brother goodnight and closed her eyes to sleep. The idea brought comfort, but the way Jesus said it, made her uneasy. There was a quiet tone of finality just beneath the words.

I will see him again.

TWENTY-EIGHT

Everything changed. Mary woke to find her little home bustling with excitement. Jesus and his men had already left for the village of Ephraim north of Bethany. Before she had a moment to be sad about missing their departure, Martha gave Mary a list of things to gather for their day. They were taking more blankets and food to the hospice in Bethany.

"I hoped to spend the day with Lazarus," Mary said with a sigh.

"Then hurry and prepare. Our brother is going with us. This was his idea," Martha explained.

Mary smiled. Lazarus hadn't visited the hospice with them since the first time, and he rarely had accompanied them into Bethany for anything. She quickly gathered the blankets and took them out to the cart where Lazarus stood waiting.

She placed her load into the back and rushed to his side.

She threw her arms around his neck. "I am glad to have you back home where you belong," she cooed.

Lazarus hugged her with a strength she hadn't seen in him in years. "I have spent too much time at home already," he said once he finally released her from his embrace. "And so have you. We should be about town, telling others about what Jesus has done for our family."

Mary nodded and kissed his cheek. "Yes, brother! We shall tell everyone we see in Bethany."

"And what about our fields?" Martha asked carrying out a basket filled with fruits of their garden. "Do they tend to themselves these days?"

"Asa can manage without me for a little while, Martha." Lazarus patted their donkey on his neck. "I need for people to see me. To see what Jesus did. Especially the ones who saw me buried. They need to know the Lord's power."

Martha clicked her tongue and looked back at the house. "There is enough trouble for Jesus already. He has barely escaped being stoned and beaten more than once. Powerful people want him silenced. Do you really think this will help his cause?"

Vera brought a second basket filled with bread. "Is this enough, Mistress?"

Martha took it from her and nodded. "Yes, thank you. Will you be all right here alone?"

Mary and Lazarus watched their sister deliver the same instructions to Vera as any other day, with one exception. When she was finished, she kissed Vera on each cheek. "Thank you, dear. You are a blessing to our home."

"Your home is a blessing to me," Vera replied and went back to her chores.

"Are we ready, then?" Lazarus asked the women.

Mary shook her head and tugged on her long black curls. "I have to wrap my hair. I will only be a minute." She ran inside and snapped up her comb and head scarf. She shrugged at Vera, who was already back to work. "I cannot have this flying wild in the wind." She quickly pulled the comb through her hair and began the careful process of wrapping and turning until every curl was covered and secured within the scarf. She tossed her comb onto her bed and waved to Vera. "You are a blessing."

When she joined her siblings at the cart, Martha shook her head. "Is this," she gestured to the scarf, "vanity or modesty?"

Mary pulled at the wispy curl escaping Martha's head wrap. "I could ask you the same." Lazarus clucked at Mary's quick wit.

As the three walked toward the village, Mary noticed a few small crates in the back of the cart. "What are these?"

Lazarus laughed, and the deep rich sound surprised Mary. She almost expected him to start coughing as he had when he first became ill. "These are some of the gifts brought to us when I died."

The words fell heavily on her heart. *Her brother had died.* To have him back again had almost erased that nightmare from her memory. Almost.

"I tried to return them, but of course, our friends are too generous and would not accept." Lazarus wrapped his arm around Mary's shoulder. "Since I am no longer dead, I thought perhaps they might better serve others less fortunate."

Mary's heart swelled, and tears filled her eyes. Before Lazarus died, he would have kept the gifts for the family out of concern for what the future might bring. Now he seemed to think more of what he could give rather than save.

Martha glanced over at Mary with a smile that indicated she felt the same joy at Lazarus's change.

When they arrived at the hospice, Lazarus maneuvered the cart close to the front door. Mary picked up her stack of blankets and rapped on the heavy door. By the time Martha had the baskets of food ready, the nurse had appeared.

"More? But your family is in need," she began to say, but then she saw Lazarus approach. Her jaw dropped, and her hands flew to her cheeks. A sharp, short scream erupted before she could clasp her fingers over her mouth.

"Do not be alarmed," Lazarus said. "I am alive and well."

"But how?"

Mary wanted to answer, but a broad smile was all she could produce. Martha leaned forward and whispered, "Jesus of Nazareth."

The nurse composed herself and managed to take the baskets from Martha's arms. "I see," she said, though it was plain to Mary and the others that she did not.

Two more women came to the door to see what had caused the clamor, and both reacted similarly.

After a few seconds of gawking and disbelief, Lazarus nodded to the crate in his hands. "May I come in? We have many gifts."

The first nurse shook her head. "There is disease here."

Lazarus laughed again, and Mary realized how much she had missed his laughter. "Woman, I was dead for most of this week, and Jesus raised me and gave me back my life. I do not think any disease you have here will trouble me in the slightest."

Now Martha laughed, and Mary's bliss was complete. The nurse allowed Lazarus inside while Mary and Martha waited at the cart.

They watched as the village market began to buzz. People had seen them, and they paused for a quick *Shalom* as they passed. The sisters were accustomed to people whispering around them, but not in a friendly way. This was different.

From across the road, a familiar face appeared. Their friend Simon approached with a broad smile and his arms outstretched toward them.

"My sisters!" he called out. "I heard the news that you were at the market today." He greeted each woman with a kiss. "Where is Lazarus?" He looked at the door to the hospice. "He is not ill again?"

"No," Martha replied. "He brought some gifts." Martha smiled at Simon with her whole face, and Mary noticed.

"I heard that he had died," Simon began. "Then Jesus came. I knew that everything would be right."

Mary nodded. "We thought it was too late. But Jesus brought him back."

Simon pushed away a tear and looked into Martha's eyes. "I was away, north of Jerusalem, when it all happened. I would have been here if I could."

"I understand," Martha answered.

At that moment, Lazarus joined them, and Simon embraced his friend with a hearty laugh. "Ahh, what the Lord has done for us!" he said.

Martha took a deep breath and smiled. "You must come and visit soon, Simon."

"Yes, yes, my friend," Lazarus agreed.

Simon clapped his hands together and raised his face to the sky. "Such blessings! This is why I rushed out when I heard you were here. I have come to invite you all to my home for supper on the first day of next week. We will have a grand celebration. You all must come."

Mary looked to Lazarus for permission, and he looked to Martha. Martha tucked her chin demurely and smiled at Simon.

"We would be honored to come," Lazarus said.

As Simon left them, Mary leaned close to Martha. "He is a good man, sister."

Martha smiled and then paused as if a strange thought suddenly occurred to her. She blinked for a second and then asked, "Would you like Lazarus to speak to him about your dowry?"

Mary gasped. "No, Martha, not for me. I think he would make an excellent husband, but not for me."

Martha appeared confused. She looked at Lazarus and back to Mary.

"Martha, Simon is fond of you," Lazarus explained.

Martha shook her head and scoffed. "I will not marry. Do not tease like that."

Mary raised her brow and exchanged an amused glance with her brother. "We shall see."

The three spent the rest of the morning in the market, and the rest of the week traveling anywhere they could find people to tell about Lazarus's miracle. The morning before the Sabbath, they went to Jerusalem to see Tirzah and Nicodemus.

Tirzah could only visit for a few minutes, as Gad and Omar were home, preparing for their next journey.

"I heard your news," she told Mary. "For a moment, I doubted, but I remembered how much our Lord loves you. Then I knew it was true."

Martha nodded. "We are filled to overflowing, but truthfully, I am worried to be here in the city."

Tirzah looked around the marketplace. "Maybe you should be concerned. I have heard troubling things. Jesus has upset many people. There is unrest everywhere. I have heard rumors, but I do not want to worry you more."

"What is it?" Mary asked.

"Your brother." Tirzah patted Lazarus's hand and turned to face him. "I have heard your name mentioned as the men grumble. While this miracle may be a triumph in Bethany, it is quite a problem here in Jerusalem."

"I wondered. But what choice do I have? I was dead. Jesus raised me to health. I cannot hide the facts. I cannot be silent, even if I wanted to." Lazarus shrugged and then gestured to his sisters. "My only fear is for them."

Tirzah nodded. "Take them back home. Trouble is coming; I feel it." She gestured to the Roman soldiers posted at the perimeter of the square. "People meet in quiet corners, trading secrets for silver. Important people who should have no need for shadows. And soldiers are everywhere. Best to get home soon. Passover is coming, and things will only get worse. Stay in Bethany."

Mary swallowed hard. She loved Tirzah, but right now her friend was scaring her. "We miss you."

"I will visit soon," she said. She kissed Mary's forehead. "I will visit soon."

Mary watched her walk away with Josiah at her side. An ache pushed its way into her heart. She didn't like this change at all.

They strode the other direction, toward the Damascus Gate, where they were to meet Nicodemus. He stepped out from around a corner as they approached.

"I am glad to see you, dear friend," he said as he embraced Lazarus. "I wish you had not come, though. It is far too dangerous for you."

"What can anyone do to me?" he answered.

Nicodemus shook his head. "You are not indestructible, brother. We have already established that." He looked over his shoulder as if afraid someone was watching. "You are a threat to every establishment in this city."

"How can I be a threat?"

Mary wondered the same thing. Her brother was the kindest man she had ever known besides her father. He would never hurt anyone. She struggled to understand.

"You are living proof," Nicodemus said. He grabbed Lazarus's shoulder and shook it. "In the truest sense of the word. You were dead and buried. Four days in the grave, with dozens of witnesses. People cannot deny it as a hoax or dismiss it as a legend. You are proof that Jesus is more than a prophet or a teacher. You are proof that he is more than a man."

"He is the Messiah," Mary blurted out.

"He is," Martha added. "You know it as surely as we do."

Nicodemus grimaced. "This. This is what I mean. This is what people are saying, and this is what could get you killed."

"They cannot kill my brother," Mary insisted. She took Lazarus's hand and held on as if her own life depended on it.

"They can," Nicodemus said.

"Who?" Lazarus finally asked. "Who wants me dead?"

Nicodemus stared at the ground for several seconds before making eye contact again. "It is more than just one group. Jesus speaks of this kingdom to come. Anyone with any power, or aspirations of power, feels threatened by him."

"I cannot hide." Lazarus looked at both Mary and Martha as if he was apologizing. "But I will return home. There is no need for you to be implicated by being seen with me."

Mary watched as Nicodemus dropped his shoulders and walked closer to the gate. "I want you all to know that I do believe, but I would lose my place on the council if others knew. As long as I have my station, I can hear news of their plans, and those of others. Perhaps I can warn you."

"Yes, friend," Lazarus whispered, "perhaps you can."

The day of Simon's feast had finally arrived. Mary put on her best tunic and wrapped her hair in her favorite scarf. She noticed Martha taking extra care with her hair and her veil. Lazarus had gone out early for water and had already returned, bringing Asa back with him.

Vera finished with the day's bread and then worked on a batch of honey cakes for the supper.

"All three of you look lovely," Lazarus announced when he arrived. "Asa and I will load the cart while you finish your preparations."

Mary watched as the men packed the small wagon with the full water jars, as well as baskets of fruit, bread, and the honey-cakes. "Such a feast," Asa remarked. "And you are not even the host."

"Martha insisted."

Mary pretended to study the contents of the cart. "I think she would like to host a celebration with Simon."

Lazarus waggled his finger in Mary's face. "You should tend to your own business." He raised a brow and leaned closer to her ear. "Just between us, I believe you are right. And what is more, Simon has asked to speak to me after supper."

Mary's heart leaped for joy. "What a blessing!"

Lazarus held up his hands and scowled at her. "Do not say a word, girl."

"I can keep a secret, so long as you tell me tomorrow what he said." She twirled in a circle in front of the cart, and her dance seemed to make the donkey nervous.

"If I can," Lazarus promised.

"What can you do?" Martha asked as she joined the others.

"He can do anything," Mary said, still twirling.

Martha rolled her eyes at her sister and put another basket into the cart. "Olive dip," she explained.

Vera walked out of the house with a bundle under her arm.

"And what is that?" Lazarus asked.

Martha shook her head. "You will see later."

Mary stopped her twirling and ran back into the house. "I almost forgot," she said when she returned with a small package in her hands. Before anyone could ask, she tucked it into the pouch at her waist and shrugged. "I can keep a secret."

As they walked the road to Bethany, they were joined by Josiah and Tirzah.

"Shalom, my friends," Lazarus greeted them. "I did not expect to see you on this road today."

Tirzah exchanged a glance with Vera and then smiled. "Simon invited us to his celebration, too."

"Wonderful!" Martha said. "We have missed your visits."

Josiah nodded. "Gad and Omar are busy preparing the caravan. They will leave again after Passover." He faced Lazarus and lowered his voice. "Are things well with you?"

Mary skipped up beside the men. "We are well. Why do you ask?"

Lazarus pointed a sharp gaze at her. "You know why he asks." He nodded to the young man. "We have heard many troubling things, but we are fine."

"The city is like a field of dry chaff. One small spark and the whole thing will burn. On one street you can hear people praising Jesus. On the next they curse him. And this week I have heard your name come up in both conversations. I fear for you and your sisters." Josiah placed a firm hand on Lazarus's shoulder.

Mary started to speak, but Lazarus interrupted her. "Do not fear for us, my friend," he said. "The kingdom of God is at hand. Our Messiah has come, and we all must be ready for him."

Mary listened. She wanted to ask what Lazarus meant. If anyone really knew what Jesus' kingdom was, surely it was her brother. But something kept her from speaking. Somewhere in the back of her mind, she felt she knew what Jesus talked about, and it frightened her.

They all walked through the market, past an inn and a row of smaller houses before they came to Simon's home. Mary knew before they entered that Jesus was already there. The other women hurried inside to where Simon's mother waited. Simon greeted all the men on the portico and welcomed them inside.

Mary stayed with the cart as the house servants came out to unload the contents for the feast. When they had gone back inside, she lingered in the dusk of the setting sun.

"Yahweh God and eternal King of the universe, You gave me breath, and with it, I draw strength. Your love around me and Your blessings around me have surely brought me to this day." She stretched her hands upward as if she were holding the whole sky in front of her. A single star appeared just above the southwest horizon. "Lord, whatever You set before us, may we face it with courage and with strength."

"A brave prayer," Jesus said from the portico behind her.

She jumped at the sound of his voice. When she turned to face him, she could see his smile, and she hurried to greet him.

"You are here!" She embraced her friend as though she hadn't seen him in years.

"You did not come in with your brother and sister," he said, still holding her hands. "I had to search for you."

Mary lowered her gaze and gestured to the house. "I have heard people talk this last week. They say that there are some in Jerusalem who want to hurt you, and my brother, because of what you did for him."

Jesus nodded. "That is true, but you must not be afraid. This world is filled with trouble. Nothing is easy. But you have great love and compassion for others, and that will give you all the strength and courage you need."

"Things are changing," Mary said, but she meant it more as a question.

"Yes, I will not always be with you."

"I know. You will leave us soon." Her heart was breaking as she spoke. "I know."

Jesus placed his hand on her cheek and smiled. "I wish everyone understood as you do."

Mary shook her head. "It is too much to bear."

Jesus gestured to the door. "Come in and celebrate with your friends."

Mary followed her friend into the crowded house. The pouch on her sash grew heavy as she thought about what was inside.

THIRTY

Mary sat in the corner of the room and listened as Simon welcomed his guests. He called for everyone present to honor Lazarus and especially Jesus for all he had done. Mary counted, at least, a dozen people there who had been healed or touched by Jesus in an extraordinary way, including herself. She watched and smiled as Vera and Martha unwrapped their secret gift and placed a woven scarf over Lazarus's shoulders. Everyone cheered.

The whole house hummed with excitement, making it difficult for her to make her decision. She held her pouch in her lap, feeling the little alabaster box through the fabric. She had brought her most precious gift to the supper in case Simon announced his intentions for Martha. She knew that both Martha and Tirzah wanted her to keep it for herself, but with all the events of these last days, she felt less and less like it was meant for her.

Something in her heart spoke. The longer she kept it, the more she dwelled on why she had it. Letting it go meant letting it all go. She was healed. Truly healed. It was time to give the box away.

She wondered if Martha would even accept it, or if it would bring scolding in front of the whole gathering. She remembered Tirzah's words. *The value is in finding a good man on which to spend it. I believe in you. I trust that when you meet that man, you will know.*

Simon was a good man. But then so was her brother. Martha had prevented her from using it for Lazarus when he had been sick. She had even wanted to use it for his burial, but dared not ask for fear of seeming frivolous in a moment of great despair.

Tonight was different. Things were changing. She was changing. She did not need a husband if Martha had one. Lazarus was now almost a hero, and his wealth would be restored with a year or two of good crops. He would soon have the means to take a wife.

Her thoughts lingered on Jesus. Other women traveled with him; perhaps she could, too. Did she have the courage to ask? If she offered the jar of spikenard to him, would he allow her to travel with him and his men?

Before her questions could settle, a loud scream came from outside. The men jumped to their feet, and the women retreated to the small room beside her.

"Bring them out, Simon!" a gruff voice called from the road.

Simon and his father stepped to the door and opened it. A large crowd of men waving torches and lanterns had gathered in front of the house. Mary strained her eyes to see them. Some had clubs, others clutched large stones, all of them looked angry.

Simon stood square with the door and filled the opening with his whole body. Mary had never seen him look so mighty. "You are bothering my guests," he called out.

"We want the man called Jesus of Nazareth and your friend Lazarus. They are making blasphemous claims. That will not be tolerated."

Simon almost laughed. "You want them brought out because of what claims? That Jesus can heal a man of leprosy? That he can make the blind to see? That he can restore a dead man to life? Are those the claims you find objectionable?"

"Bring them out to us!" one repeated.

Mary held her breath. Everyone in the room was silent with a smothering fear. Except for Jesus. He shook his head and whispered, "Do not be afraid. They will leave soon."

The angry men started yelling curses and waving their flames violently. "Bring them out! Bring them out!"

"They are my guests, and I will protect them as long as they remain in my house." Simon nodded to his friends, many of whom positioned themselves between the door and Jesus and Lazarus.

"Then we will come in and get them!"

Mary watched in terror as a man in the front of the crowd lifted a large rock over his head, preparing to hurl it at Simon. But he stopped and dropped the rock as if held back by some unseen force. The fierce crowd of men became silent.

Jesus turned his head, and his gaze met Mary's. She thought she saw him smile. Mary remembered the psalm, "He will give his angels charge over you, to protect you," Simon held his place at the door.

"You should leave now. You are not welcome in my home," he called out.

One by one the men left, muttering and confused, dissolving into the darkness. Simon closed the door, and the whole room seemed to sigh with relief.

Mary's heart still slammed in her chest. Her decision was made.

The men all went back to their seats, reclining around the supper table. The other women returned to their places and began pouring out wine and serving the food. Mary had another task to perform.

She took a seat on a small bench against a wall and placed her pouch in her lap. She removed the alabaster box from its wrappings and offered a quick, silent prayer of dedication.

Mary held the box in her left hand, and with her right, she dug her fingernails into the hard wax seal around the lid. It made a loud pop when the airtight seal broke, and soon the whole house was filled with the aroma of the perfume.

"What has she done?" Martha whispered when she realized what had happened.

Mary didn't care. A peace settled in her heart, and she knew this was right. As she carried the box toward Jesus, he straightened himself to an upright sitting position, facing away from the table. She bowed with the deepest respect and held the box over his head.

Jesus smiled at his friend and lowered his chin to his chest, allowing her to begin the ritual.

Mary tipped the box forward and carefully poured the oil over the crown of his head. The thick perfume ran through his hair, over his shoulders, chest, back, and legs, and finally, the box was empty. As the fragrance spread, Mary pulled at her headscarf and loosened her hair. She knelt before her Messiah with tears filling her eyes. She couldn't keep them from falling and mingling with the oil that now covered his feet.

Clutching his ankles and kissing his feet, Mary could only weep and thank the Lord for everything he had done for her. For her family, for her mind, for the indescribable peace, she had in her heart. His love around her, his blessings around her, had surely brought her to this day. She knew that He was the only man to whom she could offer this gift.

As she wiped the tears and oil from his feet with her hair, Mary thought she could hear someone muttering about her.

"Leave her alone," she heard Jesus say. "She has done a beautiful thing for me. I will not always be with you, but from now on when people speak of me, they will honor her. She will always be part of my story."

Mary's heart swelled as she looked up into Jesus' face. She knew now that there would be great challenges ahead, but she also knew that she could face them with strength and courage.

THE END

About the Author

Kimberly Black is an award-winning author, designer, Bible school teacher, and speaker. She lives in the Texas Panhandle with her husband, children, and fur-babies.
She enjoys writing historical Christian fiction, children's books,
sci-fi, suspense, short stories, and her blog.
Please visit her website for more information.
www.kimblackink.com

More Books by Kimberly Black

Lydia, Woman of Purple
Lydia, Woman of Purple, Devotional Study Guide
Her Most Precious Gift, Devotional Study Guide
Pockets (children's book)
Sophie Louise Will Not Say CHEESE (children's book)